ABBIE'S
Sacrifice

A NOVEL

LEONARD ELLSWORTH DAVIS

Requiem House
TYLER, TX • BUENA VISTA, CO

Produced with the assistance of Fluency Organization, Inc.

ACKNOWLEDGMENTS

This book could not have been written without the support, encouragement, and love of my wife, Rhonda Starling Davis. Without her, I would have never been able to start, much less finish, this book. She is the best!

Having never written a book, I would have been totally lost without the tremendous help of my writing consultant, Mary Ann Lackland, CEO of Fluency. Thank you, Mary Ann, for encouraging me, pushing me out of my comfort zone, and keeping me on track. I could not have done it without you.

I would also like to thank all the preservers of history, including the great tools available at ancestry.com and hardworking and seldom appreciated volunteer local historians like the late Nancy Manley of Leadville, Colorado. Nancy wrote *A Short History and Some Letters of Judge William Kellogg*

(1844-1893) in 1995, which helped preserve important pieces of this story. Al Herrick of Plymouth, California, saved old Kellogg family letters. Janice Fox of Leadville, Colorado, helped preserve many of the old records as part of the Leadville Heritage Museum and Lake County Civic Association. Bonnie K. Goodman also wrote *The Rise and Decline of Leadville, Colorado* in 2008.

Thank you to my good friend, Rene Hughey, who was so helpful and encouraging in my genealogy research, sharing her vast experience every step of the way.

I would finally like to thank my mother and father, Virginia and Bill Davis, who in addition to being such wonderful parents held onto many old family papers, news clippings, and photos when many would have simply put them in the trash. Without their stash of old papers, much would have been lost to time.

To all who came before me.
Without knowing it, they would impact my life
and the lives of those who follow me in so many ways.

The lives they lived, the struggles they endured, the tragedies
they suffered, the tenacity with which they carried on, their
successes and failures—all made them who they were.

And in a ripple effect, they have made me much
of who I am and who those who follow will be.

INTRODUCTION

For most of my life, I knew almost nothing about my great-grandmother on my father's side. She was always a mystery to me. What I did know was limited to the simple fact that she died young after giving birth to my grandfather. Born in the late nineteenth century, Abbie Cassidey Kellogg (1873–1892) died in Toronto, Canada.

Until one year ago, I knew nothing else about her. Nothing of her background. Nothing of her interests. And nothing of her own family: who they were, where they came from, where they lived, or what they did for a living. In contrast, my father and grandfather had always told many stories about their side of our family. They shared little or nothing about the Kellogg family, as if some branches in the family tree were missing, or unknown, or not to be discussed.

The lone piece of information I had about some of those missing branches concerned an oil painting that I inherited when my parents passed away. It was a simple cliffside seascape in a crude wood frame, and it had bounced around from home to home for generations. The painting apparently occupied my grandparents' home for several decades, then gathered dust for many years in my parents' closet before coming to rest with me in in our home in Tyler, Texas.

The painting had seen its fair share of family history—a silent witness of all that had transpired over many years and generations. When my wife, Rhonda, and I retired and moved from Texas to Buena Vista, Colorado, I came across the painting again while rifling through leftover boxes of odds and ends we'd set aside during the move. To this day, I don't really know why I took that family heirloom out of a box and took some time to give it a good look. It wasn't a bad piece of art, I decided. It even had a haunting quality to it, with muted colors and storm-laced clouds depicting a melancholy scene of a sea-washed cave burrowed into the heart of a cliff. Two silhouetted figures on the edge of the cliff gazed off into the distance, as if searching for something on the horizon.

After showing it to Rhonda, I took the old painting to a shop in town, had it reframed, and then started looking for a place to hang the piece in our home. We tried several spots before agreeing that it looked best over our fireplace. Looking back, I wonder now if the then anonymous, long-dead painter had been quietly seeking a definitive place of honor for the work and was pleased that it finally found a home.

As I was hanging the art, I noticed a name and a date from 1890, thinly scrawled diagonally in the corner of the painting. The writing was almost imperceptible, bobbing like a piece of fishing line in the blue-green waters of the ocean. I stared at the revelation of a name I knew but had never seen before on the painting: *"Abbie Kellogg - November 27, 1890."*

My eyes then wandered to the opposite lower left corner where the cryptic words, *"Fingal's Cave, Staffa"* were noted in the same feathery handwriting. I had never heard of this place, but the strange cave kept entering my thoughts. A few nights later, I stayed up a little later than normal, searching the Internet for "Fingal's Cave, Staffa." I was stumped to learn that Fingal's Cave is a part of the Inner Hebrides of Scotland, a chain of islands that included the uninhabited island of Staffa.

To my knowledge my family had no known association to Scotland, but it struck me how she had portrayed this random sea cave with such familiarity. Had she and my great-grandfather been there before? Was it a favorite destination? Seeing Abbie's name with a curious tie to Europe awakened something in me that I did not know was there—a desire to find the long-missing pages in my family's history.

But where to start? It wasn't an easy journey. I quickly logged hundreds of hours researching old family letters, visiting libraries, and reading Wikipedia pages, and ancestry.com. I began filling in some of the gaps of a story that I'd only heard bits and pieces of before. When I learned that Abbie's family had moved from Illinois to Leadville, Colorado, in 1880, I was sitting at my desk in Buena Vista, less than 30 miles away. I could not believe that I somehow ended up living in the same Arkansas River valley as my unknown ancestors, surrounded by the same mountain peaks, traveling the same routes, and perhaps even fishing the same river. Then I learned that Abbie's father, my great-great-grandfather, had served as a prominent attorney and judge in Leadville. In fact, he was the only attorney to ever prosecute Doc Holliday in court. I was dumbfounded. I had always thought I was the first attorney and judge in our family, but not so.

When the full story finally started coming together, I realized something else about my great-grandmother. Although Abbie Kellogg died at a young 18 years of age, her short life had set a much longer story in motion and one that is as mysterious as it is intriguing. The more I researched, the more I uncovered timely coincidences, crippling heartaches, wild adventures, and fateful decisions that no one in my family had even talked about for generations. These events had shaped not only my ancestors, but also my own life in ways that I could not have foreseen. This is that story.

Leonard Ellsworth Davis
Buena Vista, Colorado
Fall 2023

THE FAMILY TREE

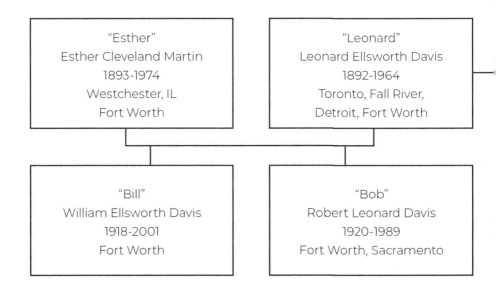

"Esther"
Esther Cleveland Martin
1893-1974
Westchester, IL
Fort Worth

"Leonard"
Leonard Ellsworth Davis
1892-1964
Toronto, Fall River,
Detroit, Fort Worth

"Bill"
William Ellsworth Davis
1918-2001
Fort Worth

"Bob"
Robert Leonard Davis
1920-1989
Fort Worth, Sacramento

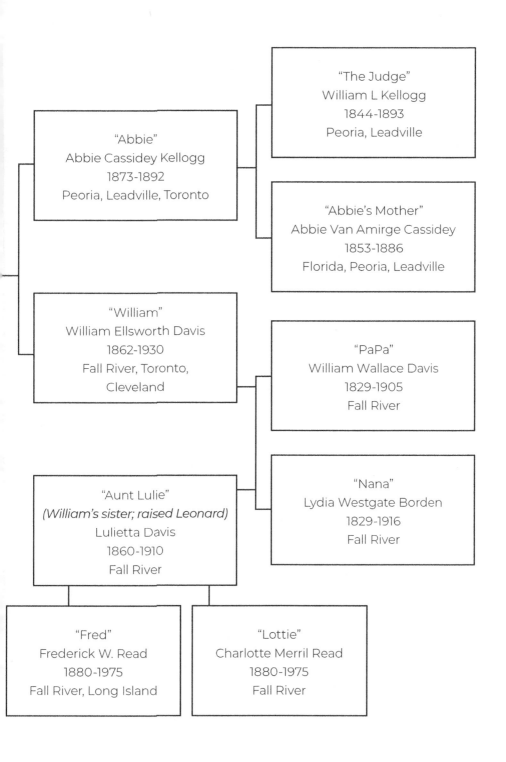

"Abbie"
Abbie Cassidey Kellogg
1873-1892
Peoria, Leadville, Toronto

"The Judge"
William L Kellogg
1844-1893
Peoria, Leadville

"Abbie's Mother"
Abbie Van Amirge Cassidey
1853-1886
Florida, Peoria, Leadville

"William"
William Ellsworth Davis
1862-1930
Fall River, Toronto,
Cleveland

"PaPa"
William Wallace Davis
1829-1905
Fall River

"Nana"
Lydia Westgate Borden
1829-1916
Fall River

"Aunt Lulie"
(William's sister; raised Leonard)
Lulietta Davis
1860-1910
Fall River

"Fred"
Frederick W. Read
1880-1975
Fall River, Long Island

"Lottie"
Charlotte Merril Read
1880-1975
Fall River

TORONTO, CANADA - 1890

William Ellsworth Davis had an agonizing decision to make. With firm determination and a heavy-hearted sigh, he signed the letter and laid down the steel fountain pen on his wooden desk. In the art of correspondence, a pen with self-contained ink was a recent and much-appreciated improvement of the late 1800s. It avoided messy smudges from dipping into an inkwell, but the convenient innovation did little to quell his misgivings about what he was about to do.

He folded the letter, sealed the envelope, and addressed it to a residence in Fall River, Massachusetts. William planned to drop it in that day's post. With any luck, the letter would make its way in due time from his home in Toronto, Canada, to the home of his sister Lulietta, Lulie for short. Upon receiving his letter, it would then be Lulie's turn to make an equally difficult decision. Her answer had the potential to shape the rest of their lives forever, not to mention the life of the tiny newborn baby boy sleeping peacefully in the room next to William.

Stealing a silent glance at the one-week-old child from the doorway, William found himself reminiscing. He recalled events that seemed as if they had occurred in another lifetime to another young man, not to him. How had his life come to this point at such a young age? When did things go from near perfect to a near disaster? How long had it even been since the child's mother, Abbie, had left them?

The past held a blur of sorrowful and cherished memories, starting with William as a 28-year-old man running into Abbie one day on the streets of Toronto in the late 1880s. Only 17 years of age, she was equal parts playful girl and not-quite-woman. And she was beguiling.

⊷⊶

PROVIDENCE, RHODE ISLAND 1882

Before meeting and marrying Abbie, William grew up in Fall River, Massachusetts, in a blue-collar neighborhood. His mother was Lydia Borden Davis. Lydia's mother, Hannah Borden, was credited with having woven the first cotton cloth by power loom in the Western hemisphere. She made it in the factory owned by her father, Joseph Borden, in Westport, Massachusetts.

In contrast, William's dad was a laborer. William Wallace Davis worked as a sometimes-carpenter and sometimes-farmer who instilled a solid work ethic in his children. It seemed to William that his father could make anything with his hands, and he'd spent countless hours in his dad's workshop watching him work. William's brother was also a laborer, but William set his sights beyond the trades. He enjoyed school and dreamed of going on to college.

Having done well in his studies, William found himself with a unique opportunity after graduation to attend Brown University in Providence, Rhode Island, partly on scholarship and partly due to the generosity of his grandfather Joseph Borden. Brown became one of only seven colleges in Colonial America when it was founded in 1764. Now more than one-hundred years old, Brown was a leading university with an Ivy League reputation to uphold. The school was well known for producing students who were well-prepared for a multitude of careers, from civil engineering to law, medicine, and agriculture. At that crucial time in American history, graduates in those fields were exactly what was needed. America was growing and it needed leaders to take it into the next century.

By the time William completed his education, having received his degree in electrical engineering in 1882, America was just over 100 years old. The nation had moved well past the cruel ravages of the Civil War that had almost split the young country in two. Born in 1862, William was only a few years old when General Robert E. Lee, the leader of the Confederate Army, signed articles of surrender at the Appomattox Courthouse in Virginia in the spring of 1865. Although he was not old enough to recall the bloodshed that had engulfed every American family in the North and South, William had been told cruel stories of brother fighting against brother, neighbor against neighbor.

William was excited to do his part to help in the rebuilding of America and hoped his efforts would ensure a great and peaceful future for all. It was a new day, and the nation's troubled past was overshadowed by the growing optimism ushered in by recent innovations in manufacturing, transportation, and agriculture.

Electrical generation and distribution were brand-new industries sweeping North America, and William felt he was on the cutting edge. Since Thomas Edison's landmark 1880 patent of the electric light bulb, the nation shared a vision of every business and home being powered by electricity. As fate would have it, Edison's first business venture outside of his New York headquarters happened to be a generating station in Fall River, Massachusetts in 1883. When William graduated from Brown, he was offered and accepted a job as an employee of the Edison Electric Company. But he was assigned to company headquarters in New York, one of the first metropolitan cities to put Edison's invention to work en masse and install streetlights.

William began his career with Edison Electric as a foreman installing lighting systems in the textile factories in New England so that their work could continue around the clock. He was soon promoted to superintendent, overseeing the conversion of steamships to include electric power. He traveled up and down the Eastern seaboard for his work from New York, to Georgia, to Florida, and even Cuba.

William did so well that Edison asked him in 1887 to take over the Standard Oil project that sought to bring electric power generation to all its pumping stations from the Atlantic seaboard to the Great Lakes. Another promotion brought William up to Toronto, where Edison put him in charge of the company's expansion north, eventually naming him District Engineer for the Edison Electric Light Company for the Dominion of Canada. The endeavor was a meaningful career move with significant responsibilities for a young man in his twenties. But even William didn't realize how important the decision to move to Canada would prove to be in other aspects of his life.

Cold winters in Fall River as a child prepared him for harsh Canadian weather. William already knew how to deal with the huge snowfalls that piled up regularly on sidewalks and streets. But springtime in Toronto was glorious. The pink cherry blossoms in full bloom in High Park in the spring and the beautiful trees in autumn made it worthwhile living in the capital city of the Ontario province.

In the spring and summer, William enjoyed weekend strolls by the Toronto waterfront, looking out at the endless blue water of Lake Ontario. On clear days he could see the Toronto Islands and daydream of taking a lazy scenic trip to their shores. Construction had been booming in the city as it approached the turn of the century. Seven stories tall, the Beard Building was the tallest in the Toronto skyline, but it would soon be replaced with skyscrapers that boggled the mind. And the bustling Distillery District kept Canadians across the country flush with opportunities to drink good Canadian whiskey and enjoy life to the fullest.

The population of Toronto rapidly increased throughout the late 19th century, attracting industry and commerce to the waterfront harbor town, along with immigrants and educated workers alike. Three railroad companies built lines to Toronto, fueling a booming economy in a city that was bursting with activity night and day.

However, for all this excitement, William was single and increasingly lonely. Women were not admitted to Brown University until many years after William graduated, so he'd struck out there. Besides that, none of the eligible ladies he had met in all his travels up and down the East Coast had captured his attention beyond a date or two.

After living and working in Toronto a few years, William was approaching 30 years of age. He had a promising career and a stable future in electrical engineering as an engineer of distinction. But he couldn't help but wonder when or if he would one day meet a nice Canadian woman, fall in love, marry, and start a family. If she was of French descent, as many of the first European settlers of Canada were, William supposed that he might even have to learn the French language. But that would be a small price to pay for finding a good wife, he told himself. Still, nothing had happened so far, and William was only getting older.

◦‣▬◉ ◉▬‣◦

TORONTO, CANADA 1890

One day when Abbie Kellogg was returning home from the general store near her grandfather's house in Toronto, she dropped a sack of apples, spilling the red fruit onto the sidewalk. She was thankful when a nicely dressed gentleman stooped beside her and helped her gather the apples back into the torn bag.

"Silly me," she remarked off-handedly to the young man, embarrassed at having caused a scene. "This kind of thing is always happening to me."

"What is that accent?" the young man thought to himself as he helped the girl with her groceries. "If I didn't know better, I'd say she sounds American." And she was pretty too.

"Are you from the States?" he asked Abbie. "It's good to hear someone from home, isn't it?" He laughed. Abbie liked his laugh.

"William," he introduced himself, holding out his hand to shake hers. "My name is William E. Davis of Fall River, Massachusetts," he added with a certain sense of formality.

Abbie took his hand in hers and noted how warm it was. She could tell he was older, but not by so much. Abbie looked older than her years and no one would guess she was not even 18 yet. She held his hand and introduced herself.

"Abbie Kellogg of Leadville, Colorado," she said, "by way of Peoria, Illinois."

"Pleased to meet you, Miss Kellogg," William replied.

"Likewise," Abbie agreed then added, "And so, Mr. Davis, what does the 'E' stand for, may I ask?"

"Ellsworth, ma'am," William answered, suddenly noticing smudges of what looked like green and blue paint on the young lady's fingers.

"Ellsworth…where did that come from?"

"Oh." He chuckled. "My parents were great fans of General Elmer Ellsworth." William then explained General Ellsworth was the first Union officer to die in the Civil War while removing a Confederate flag from the roof of the Marshall House Inn in Alexandria, Virginia.

"Well, it's quite a name" Abbie responded.

Noticing him staring at her discolored hand, she blushed quickly and pulled back her hand. She had forgotten to wash the paint off from earlier that afternoon. Like usual, she'd been in a hurry finishing her artwork before heading to the store with a list of what Grandpa Jesse needed. She loved to paint on the canvasses she'd set up in her grandfather's attic and could often lose herself for hours in her art.

Abbie was a mess more often than she wanted to admit, but usually she didn't care about her appearance. Why should she? Abbie never dreamed she would ever meet anyone interesting on the streets of Toronto. Certainly no one like this young man. Today was a pleasant surprise.

William walked her home that afternoon and they chatted like old friends. She learned he had attended Brown University, a fancy school on the East Coast that she'd heard her father mention in the past. He had moved to Toronto from America and was working his way up in the electrical engineering department at the Edison Electric Company, William explained.

Father would be impressed, Abbie couldn't help but think, as she listened to William talk about his work. Electricity was a convenience that only the wealthy could afford at one time, but it was becoming more common in the bustling city of Toronto. The 20th century was around the corner, and the whole world seemed to be re-inventing itself every year with new-fangled modern amenities.

The young couple parted ways when they arrived at Abbie's grandfather's house. That night as Abbie got ready for bed, she replayed bits and pieces of their earlier conversation in her head. Those eyes. William had such piercing eyes, she decided, wondering if she'd ever see him again. She did not have to wonder long.

To her delight, William stopped by her grandfather's house the following weekend and asked his permission to take Abbie on a walk. Her younger brother, Willie, snickered, and her older sister, Pauline, giggled like a schoolgirl when Abbie briefly introduced William to them. Abbie gritted her teeth and wished for the hundredth time that she lived on her own away from everyone and everything.

She felt trapped and in her more dramatic moments wondered if she was truly destined to be a spinster, banished to the wilds of Canada. There she would live forever with her brother, sister, grandfather, and his wife that she hardly knew. Worse yet in Abbie's mind was the fact that if she left Canada her only recourse would be to return to the harsh realities of the frontier mining town of Leadville where her father still resided.

Over the coming months, however, the future brightened for Abbie. There were more walks and talks with William. They became good friends, and soon they were falling in love. William assured her that he understood how she felt when she complained about her life in Toronto. It wasn't ridiculous to him at all that she was dying to see the world that existed beyond the front porch of her grandfather's house. William felt the same way and they developed a kindred wanderlust to explore the world together.

When William proposed marriage, Abbie didn't hesitate and quickly said yes. They planned a day in late November to marry and get started on their new lives together. Although Abbie would be barely seventeen when she married, her wedding day couldn't come fast enough. But first she had to tell her father and grandfather that she and William planned to marry. Both gave their blessing, with her father offering to make the long, arduous trip from Leadville to Toronto to give his daughter's hand in marriage.

William was all smiles gazing at the radiant face of his beautiful young bride as they stood side by side in Grandpa Jesse's house on their wedding day November 27, 1890. Her grandfather and his wife did their best to make the day special with fresh flowers and a wedding lunch for family and friends who joined them for the celebration.

Everything was perfect—almost. Abbie just wished her mom, for whom she was named, could have been there. She would have helped her pick out her dress. Together, they could have planned every detail of the small wedding. What was the old saying? *Something borrowed... Something blue...*

But it was not meant to be.

◆━◎ ◎━◆

Abbie's father, also named William, felt a void inside as he sat next to Grandpa Jesse during the wedding, knowing that he made a poor substitute for his daughter's mother. William L. Kellogg was bone-tired, having made a 1,600-mile train journey from Colorado that had taken many days. Judge Kellogg had served as a District Attorney and Criminal Court Judge in Colorado's 14th Judicial District and had been a widower since Abbie's mother (also named Abbie) died unexpectedly four years earlier in 1886.

How the Judge longed for his wife to have been there, helping Abbie get dressed for her special day. If she were still alive, their family would still be intact in Leadville. His wife's unexpected death had changed everything for all of them. He didn't resent it. But everyone had to live with it.

The four years since his wife died had been sad and lonely for the Judge. If only his Abbie could see their daughter now. Looking at their youngest daughter standing next to her betrothed, the Judge reflected on how beloved he and his wife had also been at one time when they were young. Abbie and William. William and Abbie. The Judge mused at the irony. Tragedy had marked the end of one generation of "William and Abbie" and yet this wedding signaled the start of the next.

The Judge and his Abbie had married young in Palatka, Florida, in 1871 where her parents lived. The Judge was 26 and his Abbie was 17—nearly the same ages as his future son-in-law and daughter. As a beautiful Southern belle, Abbie Van

Amringe Cassidey had stolen the Judge's heart many years before. And he'd not been the same man since.

Now he felt his life closing about him, knowing that from this day forward the Judge's daughter and her new husband would be the ones to carry forward the next generation of devotion as a couple. With any luck, the younger version of Abbie and William would also be inseparable soulmates for life. But luck, it seemed, was not always on the Judge's side.

As bitter as the Judge had become about his own misfortune, he also felt a surge of optimism as these two young people stood holding hands and pledging their lives to each other. The Judge had never seen his daughter so happy or beautiful. After all they had been through as a family recently, he'd truly feared that a smile would never grace his daughter's face again. But there it was. She was practically beaming at William.

On that crisp fall afternoon, it seemed that absolutely everything awaited the hopeful couple on the other side of the exchanging of vows and the cutting of the cake. William felt a deep sense of happiness and satisfaction on their wedding day, envisioning their life together and dreaming of a whole world to explore with his new bride by his side. And babies—there would be beautiful children. The boys would have their father's eyes and the girls would share their mother's easy laugh. How were they to know how much things would change? Or when the unexpected would interrupt all their lives and that of many others?

⊷◉⊶

TORONTO, 1891

The following fall, Abbie and William were expecting their first baby, due to arrive in May of 1892. They were excited but scared. They told their families the news, and everyone congratulated them and fussed over Abbie. Although she was young, she quickly accepted the notion that she was going to be a mother, and a good one at that, just like her mother had been to her, Willie, and Pauline.

William and Abbie spent the next few months preparing for the baby's arrival, gathering blankets, clothes, and a bassinet for the newcomer. William worked harder than ever, saving every penny in anticipation of this new addition to their family.

Their Toronto friends threw them a small party and showered them with gifts for the baby. Abbie pinched herself when she and William headed home that night from their friends' place in town. The water on the shore of Lake Ontario sparkled beneath the moonlight. It was really happening, she told herself, squeezing William's hand. They were going to be a family.

Abbie didn't know for sure whether the baby would be a boy or girl, but Abbie believed with all her heart that the baby inside her was a boy. And she was equally sure of what she wanted to name him, as painful as that might be.

※

LEADVILLE, COLORADO 1891

Back in Colorado, when the Judge read the telegram explaining the news about the baby, he quietly shut the door of his law office. A grandchild. His first. Sitting down behind his desk, his eyes moistened and he cried as he hadn't done since his wife had died. For once, he allowed himself to go back in time and remember—and when he did, so many events came to mind.

PEORIA, ILLINOIS 1860s

Since the time he was a young man, Judge Kellogg had wanted to live up to his father's expectations. He did his best to do so, but sometimes fell short. His father was William Dean Kellogg, Illinois United States congressman from 1857 to 1863. Congressman Kellogg was a close friend of President Lincoln, also from Illinois, and had actively engaged in the debates over entering the Civil War. When the war was over, President Lincoln named Congressman Kellogg Chief Justice of the Nebraska Territory, encompassing all of Nebraska, most of Wyoming and Montana, parts of Colorado, as well as North and South Dakota. He served in this important position from 1865-1867. After Lincoln's assassination,

President Johnson then appointed him Collector of Internal Revenue for the Peoria District, where he also returned to the practice of law. It was here that his eldest son and namesake joined him to study law.

The Judge's father was well-connected and well-respected in Illinois and beyond, which no doubt opened many doors for his son. He even landed his son a coveted appointment to the prestigious United States Military Academy in West Point, New York, at 17 years of age. He was admitted in September 1861, only six months after the beginning of the Civil War. The young recruit did not adapt well to the rigors and discipline required at West Point and was dismissed two and a half years later in February 1864, despite his father's best efforts to persuade school officials to keep his somewhat rebellious young son on the rolls. His father decided that his son's best option was to return to Peoria and try his hand at the law profession. Most lawyers learned their profession through an apprenticeship at that time, rather than attending law school, and the Congressman's son followed suit.

The Judge took well to the study of law, and after passing the bar exam in 1865, he began practicing law as a private attorney. A few years later, he became District Attorney in Peoria, once again with the help of his father's connections. After the debacle at West Point, the Judge thought his fortunes were improving, then a few years later he *knew* they were on the day he met his future wife, Abbie Van Amringe Cassidey.

When the Judge traveled to Florida to marry Abbie in the spring of 1871 at her parents' home, they were truly in love. They returned to Peoria and began planning a family while he continued to serve as District Attorney and practice law with his father.

Illinois was a long way from the warm climate of Florida where Abbie grew up, but the Judge was born in Canton, Illinois, and grew up in Peoria. He had never considered another place to live. Illinois was home and he would raise his family there, he believed at the time. Fate had a plan in place that seemed immutable, as far as the Judge's future was concerned. But the future has a way of steering us in unexpected directions, often when we least expect it.

Just a year after their marriage, he and Abbie experienced the yaw and pitch of the two extremes of life. In January 1872 the young couple joyfully welcomed their first child, Pauline. But later that year, tragedy followed blessing when the Judge lost his father in December 1872. The loss of his father was profound. Congressman Kellogg had always been such an imposing figure in his eldest son's life—personally and professionally. Losing a father at any age is difficult, and as the firstborn, many responsibilities of caring for his widowed mother and younger siblings fell to the Judge. It was a weight he would feel throughout the rest of his life.

The burden was not made any easier by the Judge's younger brother, John, who was not always pleased with how his older brother was handling his father's estate and taking care of their mother. John and William had one sister between them, Paulina (who went by Wissie) and much younger twin sisters Lou (Lulu) and Emily (Lud). William was 20 years older than Lulu and Lud and was more like a second father to them. He loved them both dearly and maintained close and continuous correspondence with the twins into his old age.

John was another matter. He did not hesitate to express his disagreement to his mother and sisters with how the Judge was handling their father's estate. But the Judge, firmly fixed in the shadow of the towering figure of his father, took the criticism in stride and did his best to support his mother and sisters while caring for his own growing family at the same time. His mother, Lucinda Caroline Ross (1821-1900), would never remarry and lived another 25 years after the death of her husband.

The tragedy of losing his father seemed to fade even more when Pauline's birth was followed the next year in 1873 with another baby girl. They named her Abbie, after her mother. As successful as the Judge was in his chosen profession, nothing compared to becoming a father. The fresh loss of his own father helped the Judge relish the role much more. It became increasingly important to him to provide well for his family and sustain them any way he could.

By 1878, the Judge was progressing in his career. He was District Attorney in Peoria County and continued to do well in his law practice. Life was good and seemed to be getting better all the time. Their son, Willie, had been born two years earlier in 1876, and the five Kelloggs were living happily in Peoria.

But by 1880 the winds of change had started to blow across America with the ever-increasing opportunities afforded by innovation. By then, Alexander Graham Bell's telephone invention in 1876 and Thomas Edison's electric light bulb were revolutionizing the nation, leaving society in awe of the future. The second wave of the Industrial Revolution was in full swing. The mechanization of several industries made many influential Americans rich beyond their wildest dreams, while many others broke their backs as laborers employed in their service.

But in 1880 there was one way the common man could get rich quick—gold and silver. Striking it rich in mining was where the real money was. A laborer working a mine could overnight become rich if he were lucky. The high mountains of Colorado beckoned many an adventurer eager to make their fortune this way. American families on the East Coast picked up roots to try their luck and capitalize on the mining boom happening in Colorado and other western states.

The Judge began thinking that perhaps he was destined to be more than just a good lawyer and public servant. Maybe he could become one of the wealthy beneficiaries of this new day in American commerce by striking it rich in the mining opportunities out west. He yearned to do more than merely follow in his father's footsteps—he wanted to chart his own new course for the future. For the first time ever, he started thinking about leaving the comfort and security of Peoria and heading toward the unfolding opportunities in the American West. At least that's the picture he painted for his young wife when he came home from the office in Peoria one day and told Abbie about his idea of moving the family to Colorado.

"Abbie, it's the surest thing I've ever seen," he beamed, describing the latest opportunity he'd come across to invest in a Colorado mining claim.

Had his most-sensible father been alive, he may have thought his son had lost his mind, leaving what was a promising future in the law and Illinois politics for a speculative boomtown in Colorado. His wife wasn't exactly sold on the idea either. She had fears and so many questions.

"What about your mother? Will you be okay leaving her?" Abbie asked, knowing how dependent her husband's mother had become on them since his father died.

"Well, my sisters can check on her, Abbie, just as much as I can," the Judge offered. "They will take care of her, and John can check on her when he is in town." His younger brother had moved west years earlier to work with the railroads, but he kept in touch with the family. "Besides, if all goes as planned, we will have more money that we can send to help Mother."

Abbie expressed a few other concerns, all valid. But by the end of their talk, Abbie was on board, although less enthusiastically than the Judge. The Judge knew she would support him, whatever he decided to do. The kids were young enough to make new friends in a new school. It would be a fresh start for everyone.

Something inside the Judge was willing to take a chance and forego the security of home and family in Illinois, despite the risks. He quietly hoped that proving himself a success in Colorado would win the solid approval of his entire family and honor the memory of his father. It would just be a matter of time, he assured himself.

--•==◎ ◎==•--

COLORADO 1860s-1882

The history of the Colorado mining boom began with the 1860s gold rush in the high mountains near the town of Leadville (elevation 10,158 feet). The big find happened in the famed gold discovery in Georgia Gulch, named after a group of hopeful prospectors who had moved across America from Georgia with one thing on their minds: gold. When this ragtag group eventually struck gold, word traveled fast. Thousands of people flocked to the Leadville area. All of them had the same get-rich-quick ideas, and they jumped into the grueling, unpredictable work to make their dreams come true. Some did so, but many more didn't.

The gold boom did not last long. Within six years of that initial find in 1860, whatever gold deposits had been there were already depleted. Like dishwater draining out of a giant sink, the city's population sunk as prospectors and workers abandoned Leadville in search of greener pastures.

The gold mines remained virtually dormant for many years, and heavy black sand blew over the streets and sidewalks of a declining city, accumulating in annoying layers. Years passed before a hopeful entrepreneur happened to test the unique black sand and discovered it was full of silver. He managed to keep the discovery a secret until 1879. By 1880, the entire Leadville area had once again exploded with mining activity—this time, for silver.

That same year, Judge Kellogg was packing up his family in Illinois. He knew his timing was right, getting in on the ground floor of the next boom, this time silver! The gold rush days may have been gone, but the silver rush was on, and he intended to be a big part of it.

Judge Kellogg initially chose the town of Breckenridge, Colorado, the most civilized of any towns in the heart of the silver boom. The Breckenridge community was small and tight knit prior to the discovery of the treasure, but they were not blind to the unexpected opportunity that had come their way. The locals eagerly welcomed influential newcomers like the Kelloggs, hoping the Judge could help position the sleepy little town to become one of the most successful silver mining and supply centers in the entire nation.

In the early 1870s, the native population of Breckenridge had dwindled to less than 100, but by the early 1880s it had risen to over 1,600 people. And it was about to get even larger. The city thrived with activity as men of every stripe from all over America began flooding into Breckenridge seeking work. It was wild, exciting, dangerous, and fun having ringside seats to the birth of a boomtown.

After spending their childhood in mild-mannered Peoria where nothing exciting ever happened, the Wild West was something the Kellogg children had only read about in books.

The train from Denver would not be completed for another two years, so everything in 1880 came in by wagon or horseback. Abbie, Willie, and Pauline made sure to hold tightly to their parents' hands whenever they ventured into town as a family and watched wide-eyed at giant freight wagons making wide turns in the wider-still Main Street downtown.

The Judge's business interests in Breckenridge involved helping finance a multitude of ongoing mining endeavors. Over $82 million would be mined in silver throughout Colorado during the silver boom. His instincts were correct. There was money to be made, and he hoped to prosper in those opportunities.

To position himself in the middle of the action, the Judge landed a job as President of the Bank of Breckenridge and got to work. Not only did he help others' capital find opportunity, but he quietly invested his own funds and that of friends on the side. In 1880 he bought interests in various mining claims, including the Virginia Lode and Warriors Mark Load. The bank was thriving, and while he got by on his bank salary, he hoped his investments would soon pay off in a big way.

The prospects looked promising at first. The local economy skyrocketed, and the town quickly expanded to include two dancehalls, 10 hotels, and 18 saloons to entertain all the working men. Breckenridge also featured a grocery store, post office, dry goods store, the Judge's bank, and a drug store.

In 1881, just one year into the job, the Judge's doctor diagnosed him with rheumatism. He was even confined to his bed for a period that same year. The painful autoimmune disease of the joints plagued him the rest of his life, although he tried to ignore his discomfort. But the constant, excruciating pain made it difficult to work and difficult to rest. The high elevation of Colorado did nothing but exacerbate his condition and rendered him much older than his 37 years.

Each evening after yet another long day at the office, the Judge ate dinner with the family and tried to smile. But they could tell he was stressed, tired, and hurting. His middle daughter, Abbie, a sensitive soul, always offered to rub her father's feet whenever he complained of feeling achy in his joints, which was often.

Still, he wrote his family back in Illinois at the end of 1881, describing the family's life in Colorado and making a valiant effort to position their circumstances in a good light.

> *Breckenridge, Colorado*
> *December 21, 1881*
>
> *My Dear Lud and Lu,*
>
> *I came up into the mountains last night on some business and shall return to Denver tomorrow. I*

had a cold ride over the mountains at 2:00 a.m. (not oysters and wine) and am feeling a good deal the worse for wear today.

I rec'd Lud's letter a few days ago but haven't heard from Wiss yet, though I suppose the old lady is on her dignity. I left Abie and the babies pretty near crazy on the subject of Santa Claus—and all quite true.

Pauline, I think, is slowly improving and we have some hopes of ultimately curing her. Our bank is doing pretty well, as is the mine. I can begin to hope that hard work will, after a while, result in something. Abbie and the children are all scolding me because we couldn't go home for Christmas. But we couldn't, though I hope we will be able before very long to make a little visit. Love and happy Christmas to Ma and all. I enclose for each of you a little gift with the hope that this and all succeeding Christmases may be to my dear Sisters very happy and joyous.

Your Affectionate Brother,
William Kellogg

However, the more complicated truth unfolded in the next year as money became tighter and tighter in his new business venture. After the children were asleep, he often crept into bed next to his wife and confessed to her that he may be out of his league. He was no banker or miner. He was trained in the practice of law. But Abbie would always gently remind the Judge that he was whip smart and worked hard. He could do anything he put his mind to, she often told him. Abbie was so convincing in her affirmations that he had no choice but to believe her.

So every night the Judge rededicated himself to the task before him the next day at work. He would give it a full two years, the Judge promised himself, and if he could not turn banking and mining into a profitable endeavor, he could always return to his original calling as a lawyer. His name and his dad's legacy would make sure of that.

If the Judge could have peered into a crystal ball, he would have realized a shocking truth. Few at that time would have believed it could happen, but the silver mining boom behind the explosive growth in Colorado was headed for disaster and would be over almost before it started. By the 1890s silver mining, like gold, would burn itself out.

But there was no crystal ball. Perhaps it was the stress of the bank job. Or perhaps it was his good instincts. Maybe it was just the realization that time was running out and his ship had not yet come in. Whatever the reason, the Judge realized that he could not make a go of it as a banker or in mining. He decided to get out of both before the whole business all went south.

One night in 1882 he sat Abbie down at the kitchen table after the kids were fast asleep and told her that he planned to resign from the bank in the morning.

"But William, what will you do? We've been here for only two years and…" she protested initially.

He reached for her hand and squeezed it tightly. "Abbie, I'm going to go back to what I know. I'm a decent lawyer, remember?" he joked lightly.

Abbie took a deep breath and tried to smile. "Okay, well I guess I can take the kids out of school to help us pack up," she said, sounding very apprehensive about yet another move. "Your mom will be happy to have us back in Illinois anyway," she added, her eyes downcast.

"Abbie, I'm not talking about going back to Illinois. I want to stay here, I think I can make it as a lawyer in Colorado. It feels more and more like home here, doesn't it?"

Abbie, with tears in her eyes, nodded her silent approval, although the uncertainty of their future had her stomach churning.

"Well, then, you and I agree that Colorado is our place now. We'll make our go of it here. I can start a practice in town," he explained.

"And the kids can stay in school with all their friends," she interrupted, trying to be positive and supportive.

"With all their friends," he agreed, leaning across the table to give his wife a kiss. "So it's settled. I'll inform the board at the bank tomorrow."

The Judge dutifully planned to return to his day job as a lawyer, but other plans outside of his control were already in the works.

⊷▬▭⊷ ⊶▭▬⊷

Soon after he decided the family would remain in Colorado, the Judge came across an opportunity that seemed to affirm his decision to stay. The resignation of the District Attorney of Colorado's Fifth Judicial District encompassing Summit, Lake, and Pitkin counties created a new opportunity for Judge Kellogg who had served as District Attorney in Peoria for over eight years. He sought the office, and on May 12, 1882, Governor Frederick Pitkin appointed him District Attorney of the Fifth Judicial District of Colorado. The Judge breathed a sigh of relief, knowing he would have the rock-solid security of a government paycheck of $200 coming in every month to support his family.

He would have a lot of work to do. Each of the three county seats of Breckenridge, Leadville, and Aspen were 50-100 miles apart through rough mountain terrain. Still, criminals had to be timely prosecuted wherever they were jailed and regardless of where court was held. This meant the Judge had to travel to all three counties through the treacherous mountains, in good weather and bad.

Fortunately, by this time the long-awaited railroad from Denver stretched as far as Breckenridge, but reaching the other two county seats—Leadville and Aspen—required multiple days of horseback or stagecoach travel from Breckenridge. Leadville was the county seat of Lake County and was perfectly positioned in the middle between Summit and Pipkin counties. It quickly became apparent to him that Leadville was the ideal location for him to work from, not Breckenridge.

But the Judge dreaded having to tell his family that they were going to have to move yet again. If Breckenridge was the Wild West, he knew the reputation of Leadville as the Wild Wild West. How would he explain that to his wife?

Abbie did not take the news well, and he was not popular with his children when he informed them that the family was moving again. But his new position as District Attorney gave him no choice. Leadville would be much more conducive to his work, and his kids and Abbie would eventually forgive him, the Judge told himself. The family moved to Leadville in the fall of 1882. He assumed Leadville would be their home and he would spend the rest of his life making a good living for his family. But only part of that assumption would turn out to be true.

⊱⊰

LEADVILLE, COLORADO 1882

The Judge loved the high mountain peaks surrounding Leadville and the cool, arid climate in the summer months, but not so much the long, cold, winter months. At over 10,000 feet the air was thin and hard to breathe, another challenge for the Judge's health.

On the other hand, the Kelloggs eventually made good friends in Leadville and like all families do, they eventually found their own people. There were children to play with Pauline (10), Abbie (9), and Willie (6). They enjoyed neighborhood get-togethers, picnics, and Sunday lunches with friends. The children did well in school, usually making the honors list for their grades. Leadville slowly became an unexpected support system of other families and neighbors who loved and welcomed the new District Attorney's family.

Young Willie grew up in the shadow of his older sisters, tagging along with them on their walks to school and going swimming and fishing with the two girls during the summer. He had an independent streak like his father, and the two of them locked horns more and more with every passing year. Abbie was the creative one in the family, always doodling on pieces of paper. And Pauline was the dutiful older sister keeping order between the siblings.

Pauline took her role as the elder sister seriously and kept a careful eye on her younger brother and sister. She remained especially close to the Judge's mother and Aunt Lulu, both of whom lived in Peoria and wrote them often. Pauline wrote Aunt Lulu and her Grandma Kellogg many letters about their life in Leadville, and the Judge often tucked his daughter's notes inside his own letters to his mother and sisters. He stayed in touch frequently, writing updates on his family, including what money he could spare to help them make ends meet without his father's support.

Pauline dreamed of growing up and getting married one day, like all young girls her age did. But if for some reason that didn't work out, she reasoned that she could always move back to Illinois and live with her grandmother and favorite aunt. She was old enough to remember living in Peoria as a child and held a fondness for the area. In her heart she held out hope for a more civilized and quiet life there one day.

The Judge served his first term as District Attorney and was re-elected to serve again in 1884. Meanwhile, he continued to make the several days' journeys back and forth to Aspen and Breckenridge when he had to attend to criminals in Pitkin and Summit counties. As District Attorney, the Judge was responsible for prosecuting all the criminals arrested within the 14th Judicial District for violation of the laws of Colorado. And there were enough unsavory characters and criminals to keep him busy working long nights and going to work early the next morning.

For the first four years, from 1882-1886, the Kellogg family lived at 129 West Eighth Street in a large, three-story house. The home may have been just outside his means, but the Judge did not take time to worry about that. If his father had been alive, the Judge imagined that he would surely approve of how his son was providing a good standard of living for his family, even if they were living thousands of miles from home.

Whenever he came through the front door of their home at the end of the day, the Judge knew that for all his flaws he had somehow managed to do some things right. The children were happy, and his wife seemed content to busy herself with running the household, meeting neighbors for coffee, and transforming their house into a home for their brood. While life in Leadville had its challenges, the family had adapted well. Life was going as planned.

Sometimes the Judge and his wife even talked about having another baby sometime in the future. There was also a rumor in town that the Judge might be nominated for a better position as Judge of the Criminal Court of Lake County once his friend Alvah Adams was elected the governor of Colorado in 1886.

In a blink, Leadville grew to be the largest town in Colorado, boasting a population of over 20,000. Its citizens enjoyed an astonishing 51 groceries, 10 dry good stores, 31 restaurants, 17 barber shops, four banks, and four churches. It also featured 120 saloons, 19 beer halls, and 118 gambling houses, not to mention numerous houses of ill-repute and public clubs, attracting many questionable men to the streets of Leadville.

From the time he took office as District Attorney in 1882, the Judge stayed very busy prosecuting a wide cast of characters who were continually violating the laws of Colorado. Everything landed on his desk—from minor disputes like public intoxication, prostitution, theft, and recycling stolen goods, to more serious crimes involving shootings and murders that were all too common in the raucous counties of Colorado. The Judge had two or three shooting cases going all the time, as guns seemed to be the way many miners and workers chose to work out their differences. One particularly unsavory man would one day cross paths with the Judge and pen the Leadville courthouse into the pages of Wild West history.

Being at home at the end of every day brought the Judge solace. Abbie especially enjoyed sitting in the parlor with her family after dinner, playing board games with her brother and sister or reading by the fire. It didn't matter what they did as a family, as long as they were together. Pauline always made her laugh, and her baby brother could be counted on to get into some kind of trouble and irritate her father to no end. As far as their mother was concerned, the five of them were there for each other, and nothing could or would ever come between them. Who could know that the Judge's typical good fortune would soon take a turn for the worse and threaten his whole family. For the first time, his spot-on instincts would flounder, and his family's future would seem desperately uncertain.

LEADVILLE, COLORADO 1882

Leadville was an especially rough place, with tough men who didn't easily back down from a quarrel. The Judge had great success in most of his trials, and his reputation as a tough-on-crime District Attorney was growing steadily. Several years in, however, he found his hands full with a new challenge. In 1885 the Judge was set to prosecute a well known young 30-year-old character by the name of John Henry Holliday, better known as Doc Holiday.

Doc Holliday had arrived in Leadville the same year as the Judge—1882. By education, Doc was a dentist, but he didn't come to Leadville to pull teeth. He had given up dentistry several years before. The streets of Leadville were flowing with money, and Doc loved what he considered to be the gentlemen's game of wits. Gambling required a certain kind of mastery that was equal parts mathematics, psychology, and sheer luck. It was a lot more fun than dentistry, but it was also riskier—and a lot more dangerous.

That Doc ended up an outlaw and a gambler was surprising, given that Doc had grown up in a good home in Georgia where his father was mayor of their small town. He received a classical education, which led him to enroll in dental college where he graduated at the age of 21. He first set up practice in Georgia, but Doc's wanderlust led him to dabble in dentistry practices in St. Louis, then to Atlanta, then Dallas, and finally Dodge City, Kansas.

But at each location, he quickly became bored with his dental practice and increasingly drawn to his vice—gambling. In Dodge City in the summer of 1878 after a card game he came to the rescue of a fellow gambler and lawman by the name of Wyatt Earp who had found himself at the wrong end of another fellow's Colt .45 pistol. After Doc intervened saving the lawman's life, the two became unlikely lifelong friends.

In 1879 Doc shut down his floundering dental practice in Dodge City for good and followed his new-found friend Wyatt to the frontier towns of New Mexico and Arizona. In 1881 Wyatt landed a job as deputy town marshal of Tombstone,

Arizona, along with his brothers Virgil and Morgan. It was a tough town with lots of cattle rustling, law-breaking, and gambling—just enough action to keep the three brothers busy.

They were charged with cleaning up the town, but the line between lawful and unlawful was sometimes a fine one. The Earp boys got in a dispute with some unethical local ranchers who were more cattle rustlers than cattle ranchers. They had been getting by with their illicit activities due to their friendship with the local county sheriff who tended to look the other way. The Earp brothers, however, didn't play that game, and it all came to a boil one hot afternoon at the end of Main Street near the OK Corral. Doc knew his friends were outnumbered five to three, so he went along to help even the odds.

A gunfight ensued on the west end of town. Doc and the Earp brothers' quick and accurate shooting took its toll on their five notorious outlaw adversaries, resulting in several deaths. Local politics wavered between maintaining law and order and sucking up to the influential power of the illegal ranchers. The unfortunate result was the county sheriff getting a formal warrant issued against Doc for his involvement in the shooting.

That's when Doc wisely figured it was time to move on. He headed north to Colorado in late 1881, eventually arriving in Leadville about the same time as the Judge and his family. As they walked the same streets, little did either man know that their destinies would soon cross paths.

Doc rented a small room in Leadville next door to the magnificent Tabor Opera House that had opened in 1879. Built in just 100 days by the mining magnate Horace Tabor, the Opera House was meant to bring art and culture to town. It was the finest opera house west of the Mississippi, hosting well known luminaries of the day such as the playwright Oscar Wilde, composer John Philip Sousa, and cowboy-turned-performer Buffalo Bill Cody. Live tigers even entertained there whenever the circus came to town.

Tabor was known as "The Silver King" and was one of the wealthiest men in Colorado for many years. However, when Congress repealed the Sherman Silver Purchase Act in 1893, he went from riches to rags almost overnight. But in 1882 when Doc rolled into town, silver was still king, Tabor was on top, Leadville was booming, and money was literally everywhere. This is something Doc liked, because where there was money, men loved to gamble. He would just help relieve them of some of their excess.

Because of his problems back in Tombstone, Doc tried to maintain a low profile in town. He did his gambling quietly and hoped the pesky Arizona warrants would never find him in the remote mountains of Colorado. However, politicians in

Tombstone were not so willing to give up on their man and eventually persuaded the Attorney General of Arizona to seek Doc's extradition from Colorado. Doc had been in Leadville less than a year before they were after him again.

In the meantime, Wyatt Earp had been promoted to U.S. Marshal. When he heard about Doc's threat of extradition, he intervened and called on his good friend Governor Pitkin for help, the same governor who had appointed the Judge as District Attorney. Earp explained to Pitkin the Arizona politics at play. He assured Pitkin that Doc was only trying to help deal with outlaws in Tombstone and assured him that Doc was no threat to the Leadville community. To Doc's relief, Governor Pitkin agreed with Marshal Earp and denied Doc's extradition to Arizona. Doc was free to remain in Colorado—and gamble—another day.

Doc and Wyatt's friendship ran deep. Nine years after Doc's death in 1887 Wyatt Earp was quoted in a news article as saying of his infamous friend: "I found him a loyal friend and good company. He was a dentist whom necessity had made a gambler; a gentleman whom disease had made a vagabond; a philosopher whom life had made a caustic wit; a long, lean blonde fellow nearly dead with consumption and at the same time the most skillful gambler and nerviest, speediest, deadliest man with a six-gun I ever knew."

Not everyone shared Wyatt's high opinion of Doc, of course. And the Judge tended to agree, as he reviewed Doc's past in preparation for a trial involving the gunslinger when he was arrested for attempted murder in Leadville. To the Judge's knowledge, it was the first (and what would turn out to be the only) time Doc Holliday was ever prosecuted in court, notwithstanding his many brushes with the law for his proficient use of a six-gun.

In the summer of 1884 Doc was arrested and charged with shooting a former police officer in Leadville by the name of Billy Allen. The case arose out of a gambling debt Doc owed Allen. Doc didn't deny he owed the debt, only that he'd had a run of bad luck and couldn't pay Allen just yet. Allen didn't see it that way, and although Doc tried to avoid Allen, he kept after Doc in a very unfriendly and threatening manner.

Doc knew that an altercation was almost inevitable, but try as he might to avoid trouble, things came to a head on August 19, 1884. That fateful night at the Hyman Saloon Doc decided to play faro, a late 17th century French gambling card game. The popular bar was located near the Monarch Saloon where Allen worked as a bartender and special security officer. He was authorized to carry a gun and arrest troublemakers while at work. Doc was not.

Upon hearing Doc was across the street at the Hyman, Allen headed straight over. A friend of Doc's tipped him off that Allen was coming for him. Knowing he couldn't lawfully carry a gun, Doc had nevertheless placed a Colt six-shooter behind the bar at the Hyman and positioned himself at the end of the bar while he waited for Allen.

When Allen came bursting through the doors of the Hyman, Doc was standing next to a cigar case at the end of the bar. Allen had one hand in his pocket. As Allen's hand started to move, fast as lightning, Doc's hand reached behind the bar where he had stashed his revolver.

Doc fired, missing Allen. Startled, Allen spun on his heel intending to flee but tripped over the threshold and fell to the ground just as Doc's second shot tore into Allen's upper right arm, severing an artery. Doc then lowered his Colt for a third shot, but the bartender grabbed his arm and held him back, likely saving not only Allen's life but keeping Doc from a murder charge.

Allen, although severely injured, survived. But Doc was hauled off to the Lake County jail, where he sat for seven months through a long cold winter. Finally, on March 27, 1885, the case of *The People of the State of Colorado v. John*

Holliday, Lake County Superior Court, Case No. 258 went to trial in the Lake County Courthouse, a stately two-story brick building with cast stone outlining the windows.

District Attorney William Kellogg announced ready for trial for the prosecution, as did Doc's lawyer, Jonathan Goodnight, for the defendant. The two titans of the Leadville bar squared off in the biggest case of either of their careers. The infamous Doc Holliday stood charged with aggravated assault with intent to kill, a first-degree felony punishable by 20 to 30 years in prison.

As chief criminal prosecutor for the state, the Judge worked extremely hard in preparing his case. He felt confident he would win it, knowing what it would mean for his career. Considering his other escapades across the Southwest, the Judge concluded that Doc had dodged the law long enough. It was time to bring him to justice, and he wanted to be the one to do it.

⋄⊨◉ ◉⊨⋄

LEADVILLE, COLORADO 1885

"Gentlemen of the Jury," District Attorney Kellogg began on the morning of March 27, 1885, "today you will decide whether our young town will be one of law and order, or one of violence and ill respect for the law. This defendant on August

19 of last year laid a trap for his victim, our own former police officer Billy Allen. He hid a gun behind the bar at the Hyman Saloon and proceeded to deal faro, knowing full-well that Billy Allen working next door at the Monarch Saloon would hear he was there and try once again to collect the debt the defendant owed him, but would not pay."

The Judge paused for effect before continuing. "The defendant, with malice aforethought, then and there attempted to cancel his debt by killing Mr. Allen, which he would have successfully done, but for the quick actions of Big Moe Montgomery, the bartender at the Hyman. Big Moe saved Allen's life when he grabbed the defendant's gun, stopping him from firing a fatal third shot as Allen laid helpless in a pool of blood on the barroom floor. Mr. Allen had no weapon on him. He was defenseless. Yet he was gunned down by this defendant in a cold-blooded ambush."

The Judge stole a condemning glance at the defendant, prompting the jury members to follow his gaze toward the Doc's pale figure from his confinement.

"Today," he continued, "I ask you for justice—justice for Mr. Allen and justice for Leadville—by finding this defendant guilty and sending him to prison to spend the rest of his life so he cannot wreak his evil on any other person, or town, ever again."

After locking eyes with jury members, the Judge slowly turned and returned to his seat at the prosecution's table. Holliday, he was certain, would be found guilty. And he would be praised as the prosecutor who finally brought him to justice. This would no doubt be his finest hour and help his re-election prospects—not to mention the possible appointment he was seeking from Governor Pitkin for a soon-to-be-open Criminal District Court judgeship.

Then Doc's attorney, Jonathan Goodnight, rose from his seat. He paused, laid his large hands on his client's skinny shoulders, turned toward the jury and said, "My friends, I am here today to represent my friend, Dr. John Henry Holliday. He, like many of us, came from back East to make his home and find happiness in our community. Dr. Holliday is a re-spected dentist who has helped countless people over the years."

The Judge settled into his seat, preparing for a long ride. "What a crock," he thought as the defense attorney continued.

"Although he is somewhat retired from dental work, Dr. Holliday still enjoys an occasional gentlemen's game of poker, just as many of us do. And he has for the most part done fairly well at his new avocation. But, yes, I agree with the prosecutor that after a rough patch of poor luck he did owe a debt to Mr. Allen, which he fully intended to pay as soon as he was able. But that did not give Mr. Allen, a man we all know has a hot-tempered nature, the right to go gunning for Dr. Holliday while he was peaceably pursuing his career dealing faro at Hyman's Saloon."

The Judge took notes while Goodnight spoke.

"As you know, it is illegal to carry a gun in our fine town," Goodnight resumed. "And on the 19th of August Dr. Holliday was not carrying a gun on his person while peacefully at work at Hyman's. Now, that does not mean he needs to be stupid and not be prepared if trouble comes calling. So, yes, for his own self-protection Dr. Holliday had placed a Colt revolver behind the bar. But that is not illegal. In fact, it would have been ignorant for him to simply ignore the many threats Allen had made against him, especially when everyone knew Allen was authorized to carry a gun and did so."

At this point, Mr. Goodnight walked back over to his client. Gesturing at him with open palms he said, "Look at Dr. Holliday as he sits before you today. He is a mere whisp of a man, small of stature and weighing only 140 pounds after having been plagued lifelong with ill health from the dreaded tuberculosis disease. He is an ailing and frail man."

This was no exaggeration on the crafty lawyer's part. The gunslinger known throughout the southwest as ruthless looked more like someone's frail grandfather than a killer. As the Judge knew all too well, Holliday had done himself no favors moving to the high mountains of Colorado where the air was thin and had ill effects on the tuberculosis already ravaging his lungs and deteriorating his health. The Judge's rheumatism had likewise grown much worse in the high mountains of Leadville.

Mr. Goodnight continued his defense in a smooth, calm voice, "How many more years does this shell of a man have left? I can tell you one thing for sure. He should not spend them locked up in some cold, dank prison for simply defending himself from what appeared to him to surely be his own demise."

The Judge looked over at a jury mesmerized by Goodnight's presentation.

Goodnight then pointed his finger at Allen sitting in the courtroom several rows back. "We all know Billy Allen, don't we? All 210 pounds of him. A young, strong, fierce, and dangerous man, as many in this community will attest. Why was he terminated as a police officer of our community and relegated to a security officer at the Monarch? I suggest it is likely for reasons we heard this morning. On that fateful evening last August, Allen's reputation as a threatening individual preceded him as he stalked into Hyman's Saloon apparently looking to settle his score with Dr. Holliday once and for all."

Goodnight spent the next few minutes trying to persuade the jury to look at the situation from Holliday's perspective.

Allen worked next door. He was authorized to carry a gun. He came into the Hyman looking for a fight.

"These facts were well known by all, including—most importantly—Dr. Holliday," Goodnight continued.

"So when Allen burst into Hyman's Saloon with his hand in his pocket on a warm August evening, what was Dr. Holliday to think but that his nemesis was about to gun him down? Only later did we learn that Allen had no gun…or perhaps someone took it from him to hide the truth. But that does not change the fact that Dr. Holliday had every reason to believe that Allen did possess a gun that night. And that he was about to use it on him."

Goodnight then posed, "One does not normally have one's hand in his pocket on a warm evening in August, does he?"

Several members of the jury seemed to nod imperceptibly in agreement. The Judge felt sick to his stomach.

Goodnight said, "As his Honor will instruct you, members of the jury, here in Colorado we have a law called the 'no duty to retreat' precept. Simply put, it is a complete defense when one encounters and believes his life is in jeopardy from an imminent attack. And that is exactly what was in Dr. Holliday's mind as Allen came barreling through the saloon doors looking for him."

Goodnight turned to one jury member as if they were

friends. "What was my client to do? Simply wait for Allen to shoot him first?" The skilled attorney answered his own question without hesitating.

"No, he had 'no duty to retreat' and every right to stand his ground and defend himself. And that is exactly what he did and what any one of us would have done had we stood in his shoes that fateful day."

Goodnight was really hitting his stride now. "Who can say otherwise? Billy Allen may not have gotten what he deserved, but he certainly got what he asked for when he resorted to threats and force to attempt to collect a debt that Dr. Holliday fully intended to pay. This court is where he should have come if Allen wanted to collect a debt, not threatening Dr. Holliday in such a manner. I trust that by your verdict you will find Dr. Holliday not guilty and allow him to resume his peaceful and law-abiding life in our fine community."

Goodnight returned to his place beside his client. The Judge attempted to look calm while trying to hide his angst. Doc Holliday was doing his best to hide a smile.

—⸻—

The case proceeded throughout the day. Witnesses were called and examined by both able lawyers, objections were made – some sustained, some overruled. All the evidence was closed, and motions were made and ruled upon. As the afternoon drew to a close, the jury was told to return the following day for closing arguments.

On the morning of March 28, the presiding judge read the court's charge and instructions to the jury. Both sides presented their closing arguments. The jury then retired to the jury room to deliberate.

They didn't take long. Shortly before the noon hour, the Lake County all-male jury returned its verdict of "Not Guilty" on all charges. Doc was elated to finally be out of jail and planned to be back to dealing faro at Hyman's Saloon that very evening.

As the Judge was leaving the courthouse, he overheard two observers in the hallway. "Everyone on that jury knew and liked ol' Doc," one said to the other.

"Yes," his friend agreed. "He's a fun, straight shooter, that Doc. Billy has always thrown his weight around a lot more than he should have. Since nobody got killed, it just wasn't that big a deal. And maybe Billy got what he asked for, just like his lawyer said."

The Judge just shook his head at this interchange, which he was sure would be repeated all over town. Pushing open the front door of the courthouse and making his exit, he headed home. Justice had not been served, he thought, and neither had his reputation as District Attorney. It was a bitter turn of events, one of many to follow.

The Judge took the loss of the Holliday trial personally, his confidence shaken. He'd thought it was a sure thing, just as he had believed regarding his silver mining venture. But neither situation turned out like he thought they would. The Judge was about as low as he had ever been.

When he returned that evening to the refuge of his family, his wife had his favorite meal on the stove—fried chicken with mashed potatoes and gravy. He could smell it as he sat in the parlor and removed his dress shoes. Little Abbie came over and began to rub his swollen, aching feet as she often did before her mother called everyone to the table.

By the time they finished dinner he forgot all about his trial. As they were clearing dishes away, his wife surprised him by announcing to everyone, "I have some very good news. I'm going to have another baby."

Abbie and Pauline screamed in delight and gave their mom a big hug.

"Well, I don't really want one..." protested little Willie before his father reached over and playfully placed his hand over his impetuous son's mouth.

The Judge just smiled as he looked at his family. He was

indeed blessed, he thought. He may have lost in court that day, but he knew he had won where it counted the most. Once again, his good spirits returned as he held his wife's hand and pondered a hopeful future.

Doc may have escaped jail that day, but he could not escape destiny. He continued to battle his tuberculosis and declining health. Two years after his trial, he went in search of the curative powers of the mineral hot springs of Glenwood Springs, Colorado, as a last attempt at healing his worsening symptoms.

On the evening of November 8, 1887, Doc lay motionless under a white sheet in his tiny Glenwood Springs hotel room after a series of unsuccessful treatments. The nurse tending to him later gave witness to his final moments, branding them surprisingly sedate for an outlaw. She described Doc opening his eyes suddenly and looking down at the end of the bed. Instead of dying with his boots on as he'd always imagined he would in a gunfight, he seemed amused at the irony of his bootless feet now tucked under the bedsheet. "This is funny," Doc had said weakly before he closed his eyes and breathed his last.

⋯⟞◉ ◉⟝⋯

Local Leadville papers kept up with the prestigious Kellogg family, as was the custom in the day, noting their whereabouts and travels like local celebrities. Occasionally, the family rode by carriage to Aspen or Breckenridge to accompany the Judge on official business and enjoy the beauty of the area with its aspen and pine trees, streams, lakes, and jagged mountains.

The papers also took note when the Judge traveled for pleasure. Like Doc, this included his many journeys to hot springs in search of some relief from his rheumatism. As he aged, the Judge's condition worsened with severely painful damage to many of his major organs, and he was willing to try anything to get some relief. Wealthy patrons often traveled from as far away as New York to bathe in the supposed miracle waters of the West in Nevada and Colorado. One spring the Judge even traveled to Las Vegas to take advantage of the hot springs there. But he often took shorter trips to places like Heywood Springs, 30 miles south of Leadville near Buena Vista, Colorado. It was especially popular with those suffering from rheumatism disorders of aching muscles and joints like the Judge.

Socially, the Kellogg family settled into the town's upper-class routines. There were dances and parties and community functions that the Judge and Abbie regularly attended, given his prominent position in town. Theirs were familiar faces within many social circles, especially the wealthier citizens of Leadville. They even made headlines one Christmas when the Judge presented his wife with an elegant pair of solitaire diamond drop earrings, with one impressed journalist pegging the value at a whopping $450. Although they may not have struck it rich in Leadville, they nevertheless enjoyed an upper-class life, even if they could barely afford its rich trappings.

The Judge and his wife ate trout dinners with influential people, enjoying fresh fish prepared from the day's catch at the lake. The children attended birthday parties and celebrations arranged by notable families in town. They shopped the local storefronts lining the streets of Leadville and received family members for visits on occasion. The Hebrew Ladies Benevolent Association requested the honor of the Judge and Abbie's presence at their annual Purim Carnival. Abbie was a comfortable cook and effortless entertainer, and the Judge played host to dozens of fellow attorneys, politicians, and other notable figures in their home.

One Christmas St George's Church hosted a holiday celebration where they collected funds for a Christmas tree laden with gifts for the local children of Leadville. About 250 children attended with their families, and the night's events made the morning headlines. After the presents were opened, parishioners cleared the chairs from the floor and dancing began. Among the couples on the dance floor were the Kelloggs, who waltzed their way into the wee hours of the night.

At the office, the Judge continued to put in long hours in his never-ending trials of local criminals. The kids were busy at the Parish school, Pauline and her sister starred as fairy dancers in a school play, and Abbie earned top honors in most of her classes. The Kellogg family had by now endeared themselves to the Leadville community, and the community to them. Life was good, but it would all go so wrong, so quickly.

LEADVILLE, COLORADO 1886

Abbie could not wait to welcome a baby sister or brother into the family. Every day after school Abbie pressed her hands to her mother's growing tummy, feeling for a kick. Her mother would just smile and remind her 13-year-old daughter of how many weeks were left before the baby would be born.

To accommodate his growing family, the Judge found a larger home only one street over at 130 West Ninth Street. They closed the purchase of their new house in early September 1886. It was none too soon, as the baby was due in late October and the usual harsh winter months would follow soon after. Although heavily pregnant, with the girls' help, Abbie packed their belongings and slowly moved everything into their new home. By late September, the family was finally getting settled in the new two-story house. Pauline and Abbie shared a room upstairs, and Willie's room was down the hall. Their parents' room was on the first floor just off the parlor. The house didn't have indoor plumbing yet, but the Judge hoped to be able to add it soon. In the winter it was still a long, cold walk to the outhouse.

At the end of August, Abbie set up a wooden cradle in their bedroom. All her babies had slept in that same cradle, and her mind flooded with happy memories as she traced the wooden railings with her hand and dreamed of the future with their fourth child.

The day the baby arrived was a Sunday afternoon. They had all gone to church and returned home for a leisurely after-noon except for the Judge, who returned to his office to catch up on some work and prepare for a big trial on Monday. As he polished his opening statement, he knew his wife would be busy at home preparing her special fried venison and gravy Sunday dinner. The children were finishing up schoolwork in the parlor.

Suddenly, Abbie felt familiar warning pains and wondered if they were a false alarm or if they could be signaling the beginning of labor. There were several more weeks before the baby was due, but in an abundance of caution, she quietly took the hot skillet from the stove and set it aside before slowly making her way to the bedroom. With every step, the pain worsened and quickened. When she reached the bed, she laid down in hopes it would pass. It did not.

She summoned the children and sent Abbie next door to get help from the neighbor who had become a new friend after their move, while Pauline got her a damp wash cloth to wipe her perspiration. The baby was coming, but it seemed to be happening faster than when she had her other children. She said a prayer for her yet-born child and tried to remain calm.

When Mrs. Murdoch arrived, she dispatched Willie to his father's office a few blocks away. Willie burst out the front door and down the steps, running as fast as he could. In minutes he breathlessly burst into the office shouting, "Mother says for you to come home right now!" grabbing his father's sleeve.

The Judge was sitting at his desk, lost in preparation for his trial. "Slow down, Willie," his father commanded. "What are you saying? I can't leave right now. I'm getting ready for court tomorrow, son."

"Father, it's time! The baby is going to be here any minute!" Willie cried, impatient as ever with his dad. His father knew Willie could exaggerate, and sometimes he did not take Willie seriously. But something in Willie's voice convinced him that it really was an emergency and there was no time to waste. They were not expecting the baby until late October. Today was just October 4. The baby was early.

The Judge jumped to his feet, grabbed his jacket, and hurried after his son out the door and into the street, both moving as fast as they could toward home. When they arrived, the Judge hurried into their bedroom where he found his wife, white sheets twisted around her body in a sweat-soaked and bloody heap.

Mrs. Murdoch was wiping his wife's brow with a small, damp rag and whispering softly to her. Pauline and Abbie had their backs to the Judge, standing silently and stoically at their mother's bedside.

The girls whipped around at the familiar sound of their father's voice, faces ashen with anxiety. "Father!" Pauline cried. "Something's wrong with Mother."

Just then the Judge noticed that Pauline was cradling something in her arms. He moved closer. Wrapped in a blood-soaked towel was a frail little creature. It made no sound at all. The Judge stood frozen in time. What was happening? Then a baby's faint cry riddled the silent room, and he realized Pauline was holding a tiny baby. His son.

Mrs. Murdoch vacillated between tending to the mother and fussing with the bundle Pauline was holding. The Judge was stunned and trying to take it all in. Finally, he snapped to attention, patted Pauline's shoulder, and made his way to his wife's side, kneeling beside her.

"Abbie, darling. Can you hear me?" No response. "Abbie!" he cried.

Abbie seemed in a daze, unresponsive to her husband's voice. She was pale and clammy. Her eyes were faintly open, her breathing shallow. He knew immediately that this was not like her other births and his stomach tightened in knots.

Mrs. Murdoch grew more frantic, trying desperately alongside the Judge to arouse the young mother. The Judge knelt and slipped his arm behind Abbie's neck, cradling his bride to his chest. Suddenly her gaze focused on him, and a faint smile seemed to bring her to life, then she went limp again and her eyes closed.

Pauline and Abbie looked at their mother. The girls gasped and Pauline let out a soft but shrill scream.

"Mother! No! Mother!" Abbie cried, and held onto her sister, like the children they were. Willie slipped quietly out of the room, not wanting to spend another second near the horrific scene. So much blood and confusion. What was wrong with Mother? Why couldn't Father do something?

Mrs. Murdoch tried to check Abbie's pulse. She thought there was something there, but it was faint and slow.

"Where is that doctor?" Mrs. Murdoch said under her breath. She had sent her husband to get him, but that seemed like ages ago.

Knowing there was little she could do for the mother until help arrived, Mrs. Murdoch turned to Pauline and quietly took the baby from her arms. Pauline offered no resistance and Mrs. Murdoch silently and gently ushered the girls away from their mother and father to join their brother in the parlor. No one spoke. No one dared breathe.

The Judge held his wife's body and drew her closer as tears welled up and his chest began to heave. This could not be happening, not to his Abbie. He turned his face and sobbed into Abbie's pillow, his head near hers.

"Abbie, Abbie, please, I need you. The children need you… not now, not you." The children could hear their father's wails and it startled them. They had never seen him this way. He was always in control. The house remained eerily silent as they all awaited the doctor, except for the faint, stuttering breaths and occasional whimper coming from the small bundle in Mrs. Murdoch's arms.

After what seemed like forever, but was probably less than an hour, the doctor finally arrived. Doc Gibb examined Abbie first, then turned his attention to the newborn. He muttered to himself before instructing Mrs. Murdoch to get fresh sheets and cloths. She cleaned Abbie and the bed as best she could while the doctor summoned the Judge to join his other children in the parlor, leaving the baby with the neighbor and Abbie in a deep sleep.

Doc Gibb gave his assessment. The baby seemed fine for now, he assured them. Although he was several weeks premature, he thought he would be alright. The doctor was not as optimistic about Abbie.

"She has lost a lot of blood. Her blood pressure is very low, but if she doesn't have an infection, she stands a chance. The next few days will tell. Keep her comfortable and give her fluids if she will take them."

The Judge thanked the doctor and shook his hand.

"I will check back on her tomorrow," Doc Gibb added. "It's all up to the good Lord now. I have done all I can do."

After making some further notes in a small book, including jotting down the date, October 4, 1886, he then asked the Judge, "What is the name of your newborn son?"

The Judge didn't respond immediately. But after taking a long and labored breath, he said, "Leonard...Leonard is his name. His mother wanted to name him Leonard."

Abbie Cassidey Kellogg died four days later on Thursday October 8, 1886, her 33rd birthday. She was buried Saturday afternoon in a hastily purchased plot in Evergreen Cemetery on the outskirts of Leadville. Thankfully, the hard winter freeze had not yet arrived, which would have prevented her burial until spring.

⊷⊨◉ ◉⊨⊷

The entire Leadville community surrounded the Kellogg family upon Abbie's shocking death. Abbie and her family were beloved by so many. The men of Leadville Lodge of Elks, Woodmen of America, and other social societies, including those associated with the Leadville Bar, visited the Judge to console him and help plan and participate in her funeral procession and burial. The local newspaper wrote of Abbie's passing:

> The death of Mrs. William Kellogg at her residence, on Thursday night, was the bringing down of a curtain of gloom, such has rarely been seen in this locality, where she was esteemed by all who knew her. Her illness was brief, and few were ready for such a lamentable result. But a few days ago she was ripe in the legacies of good health and strength. The Reaper, however, had placed his invisible seal, and to-day she is in the peaceful embrace of death, with a husband

whose grief is unutterable and four children of tender years. In her life is to be read some of the most beautiful poetry of nature. She was s uniformly kind, generous and indulgent, a model mother and an affectionate wife. Idolized by husband and children the loss to their hearts is an irreparable one. Among Mr. Kellogg's associates, professional and otherwise, the death of this most estimable wife is keenly felt. The bar in which he has always commanded an enviable position has been prompt in the following call: The bar are requested to meet at the district court room at 11 a.m. Saturday, to take such action as may be appropriate touching the death of the wife of our brother, William Kellogg. J. B. Bissell, President Bar Association. All friends are invited to attend in the solemn rites.

After Abbie's death, neighbors did what they could to help the widowed Judge take care of his newborn son and three other children and keep the family home going. They took turns cleaning and cooking meals for him and the children. The Judge was thankful for their help and felt especially proud of how his kids stepped up and helped with their fair share of chores. As the days became weeks and weeks became months, more and more responsibility fell on the girls as they tried desperately to take care of their new baby brother, especially through the long Colorado winter. But they were mere children themselves, aged 13 and 14. Leonard was weak and small, and the doctor made frequent house calls to tend to the infant.

Finally, spring arrived, followed by summer, and it seemed as if Leonard had made it through the worst of it. But then toward the end of the summer, despite their best efforts, their baby brother suddenly became congested and a few days later slipped from their fingers and died at the age of 10 months on August 5, 1887.

The Judge and the children returned to the newly purchased plot at Evergreen Cemetery and reunited little Leonard with his mother. After the graveside service, they returned home, exhausted and filled with more grief. But their new home was a far different place than it had been less than a year before. Not only had they lost their mother, but now baby Leonard.

The Judge felt a heavy burden. Not only was he grieving and utterly alone, but he was now the sole parent of his three remaining children. School was about to start in September. Could he manage it—their schoolwork and care, his law practice, and his health problems—all on his own? He had no choice. He had to try. After enrolling the children back in school, he began another year without his Abbie, determined to do his best.

The school year did not go well. There was not enough of him to go around. The children were at difficult ages, which was challenging enough to navigate with the help of a partner. He knew Leadville was not the best place for children, especially without a mother. He tried his best, but his law practice left little time to tend to his children, not to mention his continuing health problems. And if he didn't focus on his work, how could he provide for his family, his own mother back in Peoria, and his other financial obligations? It was a quandary and there seemed to be no answer.

⊷⊷◉ ◉⊷⊷

The Judge did get a piece of good news in early 1888. Governor Benjamin Harrison Eaton had decided to appoint him Judge of the newly created Criminal District Court for the 14th Judicial District. This was something he had always wanted, but while he was glad to finally obtain the position, it did little to ease the stresses in his personal life. Life was so hard without his Abbie.

As the school year ended and the summer of 1888 arrived,

the Judge was torn as to what was best for his children. They were not happy, they were acting up in school, and he didn't have the time or patience to deal with them. He wanted the best for their future. But what was he to do? Remarry? The prospects were slim, and he had no desire to pursue a courtship even if any eligible ladies were willing to take on three children—something he doubted.

Judge Kellogg carefully considered his other options. After much thought, he finally decided that boarding school seemed the best idea, although the closest ones were over 100 miles away in Denver. He had heard good things about Wolfe Hall, an Episcopalian boarding school for girls in Denver. Nearby Jarvis Hall was a military prep school for boys with a good reputation. While he didn't like the idea of sending his children away for school, of all his bad options this seemed to make the most sense. They'd get a good education, be well supervised in a better environment than Leadville, and would hopefully prosper.

The Judge hoped Willie would learn some discipline and not end up in trouble like he had done as the young, undisciplined cadet at West Point. Pauline and Abbie would surely make friends quickly at Wolfe Hall and get a better education than in Leadville.

He'd miss them. But they would be home on school breaks

and in the summer, the Judge assured himself. And he could on occasion go and visit them. And yet he knew the children would likely not share his optimism.

He was right. In the late summer of 1888, the Judge informed them of his decision. They were dumbfounded. Pauline protested, "What have we done to deserve this, Father?" Being sent off to boarding school was something in her mind that happened only to bad kids. "Mother never would have sent us away," Pauline accused.

Abbie remained silent but cried herself to sleep that night. The thought of having to move again, and to a foreign place at that, was more than she could bear. She felt as if she were losing what little family she had left and were being sent to prison.

Willie, being younger, didn't fully understand what was happening, but he took his cues from his sisters. Nevertheless, the Judge remained resolved that this was for the best.

On a cloudy day in early September, the Judge traveled by carriage with the children to Breckenridge where they all caught the train to Denver. When the family arrived at Wolfe Hall, Abbie and Pauline clung to their father and Willie. They did not want to let go. When they could stay no longer, the Judge summoned his strength and watched his girls trail behind the head mistress down the long hallway toward their dormitory.

Willie stood wide-eyed, not fully appreciating that he was next. The Judge then deposited him later that afternoon with a uniformed instructor at Jarvis Hall. He gave his son a firm handshake and told him to be brave and to make him proud. Willie swallowed hard, dutifully turned and followed his new commander to begin his new military life.

Abbie and Pauline had a hard time adjusting to Wolfe Hall. It was large, imposing and impersonal, nothing like their cozy home back in Leadville. At dusk the building's dark silhouette looked more like a haunted house than anything they could call "home." It was certainly a far cry from where they had grown up with people who knew them, loved them, and supported them. No one at Wolfe Hall knew their story—and even if they had been told, they could not possibly understand all they'd been through in their young lives.

They felt all alone. But of course, they were not—they still had each other. Poor Willie had no one.

Every memory reminded Abbie of how life used to be when Mother was alive. But those days were gone forever. She and her sister whispered long into the night how much they wanted to be with their mother and father again. In their worst moments, the girls admitted to each other how guilty they felt about not being able to keep little Leonard alive and wondered if Father were punishing them for their failure.

It was easy to give in to sadness and guilt. They would never know Leonard's first words and never see him take his first steps. It was a lot for two young girls—losing their mother and brother in the same year—and they would carry this quiet sadness their whole lives.

Whenever her mind drifted to thoughts of the baby, Abbie often remembered his gentle cooing and the soft tuft of dark hair on his head. Her heart ached with disappointment. Why had her mother died giving birth to their brother, if he was just going to die a few months later anyway? How could God allow this to happen? It all seemed so pointless. Many times she'd promised herself that if she ever had the chance to marry and have a son, she would name him Leonard after her brother so she could keep him alive in her heart forever. Maybe that would give his death some meaning.

Abbie and Pauline did eventually make friends at Wolfe Hall, and the yearning for home somewhat subsided. They adjusted because they had no choice. The girls tended to their studies and Abbie discovered a special affinity for art class, her favorite. Something about the paint going on the canvas and the ability to create anything she wanted appealed to her curious mind. It allowed her to briefly escape some of the sadness of the past.

Abbie could dream when she painted, envisioning landscapes and seascapes of faraway places that she would likely never see, except in her imagination. Her teachers at Wolfe encouraged her love of art. They told Abbie that she had true talent, praising the various works she created in oil and watercolor. Whenever she was down, her painting always lifted her spirits and took her to a different and better place.

⊸⊶⊙⊷⊶

LEADVILLE, COLORADO 1889

Willie, Pauline, and Abbie couldn't stop hugging each other when they reunited back in Leadville at the beginning of the summer of 1889. School was out. They were so glad to be home again and planned to play outside together every night with all their Leadville friends in the neighborhood. Maybe, they thought to themselves, Father would have such fun with them at home that he would want them to stay with him instead of sending them back to boarding school in the fall.

Their expectation of returning to happiness in Leadville turned into more of a dream than a reality within their first few weeks at home. Without their mother, things were different.

Their father's health seemed to have worsened, yet he continued to work long hours and was never in a good mood. Their old friends had moved on, and they felt more like visitors in a town where they no longer belonged.

Abbie was just shy of sixteen now and Pauline was seventeen. Both girls were plagued with typical teenage angst. Willie rolled his eyes at their frequent outbursts of drama and tears that seemed to occur for no reason at all. What was wrong with them? And what made them so mad at him when he'd done nothing to them at all? If asked, one or both girls would tearfully accuse their brother of having "looked at them funny"—when he'd done nothing of the sort! With two older sisters in the house, being a thirteen-year-old boy on the verge of puberty himself was making Willie crazy.

Midway during the summer, the Judge noted how unhappy his girls seemed. Willie too was withdrawing more and more, and he was often angry. The Judge wondered again if he'd done the wrong thing in sending them away to boarding school.

If their mother were there, she would know how to handle them. But she wasn't and never would be. He once more thought of seeking another wife, but in Leadville there were few suitable candidates for a 45-year-old widower with three children. Most of the single women worked in the bars and houses of ill-repute, which were growing in number every year. Besides, he had little interest in dating anyway. He was tired and increasingly depressed, his life closing in on him in a most unfavorable way.

He was pleasantly surprised on day when Abbie showed him some of her favorite canvas paintings from school that she had rolled up and stowed in her luggage on the train ride back home from Denver. They were really quite good he thought.

He smiled and rubbed the top of her head, like he had done throughout her childhood. "I'm so proud of you," he told Abbie. "You've got some real talent, like your mother. She was an artist, like you."

Abbie's heart warmed. But the brief happiness of the moment passed, and a profound expression of sadness overtook her father's face again. She rarely saw her father at peace anymore since Mother died. All he did, it seemed to Abbie, was work. At night he coughed. She missed the younger, happier, more confident, and optimistic father she knew only a few years before. Time had not been kind to Judge Kellogg.

Willie was a growing problem. He was more cantankerous than ever, and he and Father hardly ever got along. They broke out into explosive fights over the most trivial matters all summer. Willie could not wait to go back to Jarvis Hall at the end of summer. It was a difficult life at the strict military school, but at least there he could escape from his father's disapproval and his sisters' emotional outbursts. He'd already started to make some friends and was settling into the regimented routines. But Willie's plans met with surprise at the end of August when he instead found himself sitting between Pauline and Abbie on a train heading north to Toronto, Canada, with their father.

Just a few weeks before, after supper one evening the Judge had announced that none of them would be returning to boarding school in Denver. Their spirits brightened, thinking he was planning for them to remain with him and attend school in Leadville.

Their joy was short-lived. In the next breath he explained, "I think it best for all of you to go live with Grandpa Jesse in Toronto and attend school there."

They sat in shocked silence. Their maternal grandfather, Jesse Jennett Cassidey, was a relative they hardly knew. Slowly, this latest twist of fate sank in before Willie blurted out, "Where in the hell is Toronto anyway?"

TORONTO, CANADA 1889

Grandpa Jesse picked up the Judge and the trio of siblings at the Toronto train station and loaded their belongings onto a carriage for the long ride to his house. After staying a few days at the house, the Judge left to return to work in Colorado. His children once again said goodbye to their father, a routine to which they were becoming quite accustomed.

Grandpa Jesse (1832-1908) and his first wife, Grandma Matilda (Tillie) Van Amringe (1832-1875), were their grandparents on their mother's side, but they did not know them well for many reasons. First, Grandpa Jesse and Grandma Tillie had lived for many years in Florida and spent little time with their grandchildren up in Peoria, Illinois. Second, Grandma Tillie died when Pauline and Abbie were just toddlers and Willie had yet to be born, leaving Grandpa Jesse a widower.

Grandpa Jesse moved to Canada and remarried ten years later in 1885, this time to Annie Riley (1844-1913). She was twelve years younger than Grandpa Jesse and wanted children of her own. So they raised a family together in Toronto where he was employed as a journalist for a local newspaper. Grandpa Jesse and Annie had two children, who were both teenagers by the time Pauline, Abbie, and Willie moved in.

The small home was crowded with five teenagers and two adults. The Colorado trio felt like intruders. They were accepted, but they wondered if it wasn't reluctantly, out of some sense of family obligation. It seemed inconceivable that Grandpa and Annie's two children were their mother's half-brother and sister when they were almost 30 years younger than their mother! No wonder the three siblings felt out of place in this mixed-up family. Should they really call someone their own age their "aunt" and "uncle"? It was a crazy and unsettling situation.

Besides all this, Toronto was a completely foreign country. Most of the people there didn't speak English, only French. But the kids had no choice. Toronto was now their home, and there was nothing they could do about it.

Pauline daydreamed of returning to Peoria and living with her Grandma Lucinda and Aunt Lou. Abbie dealt with her unhappiness by losing herself in her art. And Willie was ready to hit the road and try his luck at whatever. All three agreed on one thing—namely, that their father had once again abandoned them to a foreign land, while he continued to live alone in their family home in Leadville thousands of miles away.

In truth, their father was doing his best—including sending financial support to Grandpa Jesse in his letters to his children. But these letters were of little solace. The children seldom wrote their father and grew more and more distant, convinced in their young minds that their father did not want them anymore.

Abbie even surmised that the three of them reminded him too much of Mother. Maybe he bore some resentment over the death of baby Leonard. Or maybe it was just too painful to have them around, she thought. Night after night, the three teenagers remained lonely and afraid of what the future might throw at them next.

<hr />

TORONTO, CANADA 1890-1891

When Abbie met William Ellsworth Davis that day on the streets of Toronto in 1890, her luck changed. After they married, she was the first to move out of Grandpa's house. With Abbie out of the house, Pauline had felt lonelier than ever. Abbie and William had tried setting up dates for her with a couple of colleagues at William's work, but Pauline was disinterested. She was extremely picky, and Abbie felt her older sister was particularly hard on the eligible young single men in Toronto. No one seemed to be good enough, and Abbie began to warn Pauline that she would either have to lower her impossibly high standards or resign to becoming a spinster.

The truth was that since Pauline graduated from high school, she felt even more lost and out of place in Canada. She kept dreaming of starting over again back home in Illinois. In January of 1891 she wrote her Aunt Lou in Peoria, begging her once again to let her come live with her and Grandma Lucinda. This time, Lou relented and interceded on her behalf with her older brother. Judge Kellogg gave his permission and by mid-February, Pauline had packed up her belongings and moved back to Peoria, Illinois.

But what to do with Willie, who was now fourteen years old? With Pauline and Abbie gone, Willie was all alone with his grandparents and their two kids. Grandpa Jesse was old at this point, and he certainly hadn't signed up to care for an unruly boy like Willie. His grandfather couldn't handle having another teenager in the house, especially one with a rebellious streak like Willie.

By early May of 1891, Grandpa Jesse had had enough and wrote Willie's father, informing him that he would have to make other arrangements for his son, as Willie would no longer be welcome at Grandpa Jesse's home. Willie could finish out the school year in Toronto, Grandpa Jesse wrote, but after that he would have to move out.

The Judge decided moving home to Leadville was not an option for Willie. He could not imagine bringing Willie back to the debauchery of gambling and questionable characters who permeated the town. Leadville, he surmised, would most certainly lead to his son's complete ruin. Instead, he enrolled Willie in the Michigan Military Academy, a military prep school in Orchard Lake Village, Michigan, to begin his tenth-grade year of high school in the fall.

In the meantime, he prevailed upon William and Abbie to take Willie in for the summer. The Judge would somehow find a way to come up with the $500 annual tuition for Willie's education and crossed his fingers that, this time, the financial sacrifice would result in a turning point in Willie's life.

Unlike her brother and sister, Abbie felt optimistic and

hopeful about her future. It seemed to her that once she became Mrs. William Ellsworth Davis, the disjointed events of her past life seemed to make more sense. All the bouncing around from Illinois to Breckenridge, to Leadville, to Denver, and then Toronto had taken its toll. As had the many heartaches of losing her mother and baby brother. But hopefully that was all behind her now, she thought. All the goodbyes she'd endured over the past few years were now replaced with hellos to the future.

Becoming independent and setting up her own home in Toronto as William's wife finally gave Abbie some control over her circumstances. She felt loved, truly loved, and she knew that William understood all she had been through.

After returning from their honeymoon, the newlyweds got busy setting up their new home, albeit a one-bedroom apartment with a small kitchen, parlor, and thank goodness, an indoor bathroom. William's electrical engineering career had expanded, and Mr. Edison gave him more and more responsibility.

Every industry had need of Edison's lighting systems and electrical innovations, and William stayed busy with more work than there were hours in a day. He was constantly behind at the office and was gone more than Abbie wished. But she passed her time sprucing up the apartment, cooking dinner for her tired husband, and occasionally visiting Grandpa Jesse and Annie. As planned, Willie moved in with them for the summer and things went remarkably well. William treated Willie more like a grown man and expected him to act like one, and that approach seemed to work. Willie flourished that summer and was truly thankful just to be out of his grandfather's house.

Abbie became pregnant at the end of summer in 1891 about the time Willie departed for school in Michigan. Resting her hand on the baby growing inside of her, she remembered how many times she'd done the same on her own mother's belly when she was pregnant with Leonard, feeling the same sense of wonder. Although she was very young, Abbie relished having a human life inside of her and was filled with joy and thankfulness.

Since the death of her mother and Leonard five years earlier, she'd slowly realized that what had seemed broken could be made whole once more. Leonard's short life would not be in vain. If blessed with a boy, she and William agreed he would be named after Leonard. Carrying his name, this baby would live the life her brother never could. Her eyes often filled with tears as she thought of this possibility.

Mother would be so proud of her and the family she and William were starting, Abbie would often tell herself. She also thought about all she would tell her baby about his grand-mother. Abbie wanted him to know how brave and how loving his Grandma Abbie had been, even though the two would never meet in this lifetime.

William had promised to send word of their news today to her father. She wondered what her father would think when he received the telegram. Abbie hoped it would bring a smile to her father's face, although she had not seen him since the wedding over a year ago. Back in Colorado, Abbie's father was doing his own bit of soul-searching. But his conclusions were not so optimistic. The Judge no longer had his loving wife to give him perspective and confidence. She wasn't there to cheer him up and tell him that things were not as bad as they seemed. His Abbie was gone, and so were all their children. In the void of their absence, the Judge slipped further into despair. He was alone, so alone.

As time went on, the Judge became consumed with neg-ativity, listening only to his own repetitive thoughts of past failures day after day and suffering the ill health of a man twice his age. Every night when he sat down in his leather chair by the fireplace after eating another unsatisfying dinner that he cooked for himself, his mind inevitably wandered across his past. What had he accomplished? Would his father, the esteemed member of Congress and confidant of President

Lincoln, be disappointed in how his oldest son had turned out? The Judge feared the answer. He pondered relentlessly where and how it had all gone so wrong, and the questions and self-doubt were endless. More often than not, the Judge fell asleep in his chair, full of regret and empty of hope.

One morning after breakfast at the Golden Burro Café on Harrison Street, as was his usual custom before heading into the office, he felt a little better. It was a beautiful September morning and the aspen trees on the mountains were starting to show their color. Maybe today would be a better day, he hoped, even though hope rarely amounted to much anymore.

Shortly before noon there was a knock on his office door. A delivery boy brought in a telegram that read:

ABBIE PREGNANT. LATE SPRING,
PROBABLY MAY. HOPING FOR A BOY
NAMED LEONARD.

ALL OUR LOVE.
WILLIAM E. DAVIS

The Judge was surprised and delighted at the news, but he soon grew melancholy once more. Sighing as he fingered the edges of the telegram, he pondered how he could be a grandfather already. Like most of life these days, this too was bittersweet. He was overjoyed for his daughter, but at the same time he was sad that life had not turned out as he wanted.

The Judge placed the telegram in a tin box of mementos he kept on a shelf in his office, and his mind drifted once more to the past. As a new generation emerged, he recalled his own now passing generation even more.

⊶⊜⊷

PEORIA, ILLINOIS 1850

His father, William Dean Kellogg, was born in Ashtabula County, Ohio, in 1814 but lived most of his adult life in Illinois. He pursued an interest in the law and began a law practice in his mid-twenties, Davidson and Kellogg. He married Lucinda Caroline Ross at Christmastime on December 21, 1843. They were overjoyed when their first son, the Judge, was born the following year. When the Judge was six years old, his father entered politics in Peoria, becoming a member of the Illinois House of Representatives in 1849. Politics proved to be even more demanding than practicing law, and the Congressman's notable absences filled the family home.

The Congressman became a well-respected and hard-working member of the Illinois Legislature. He could foresee a future in politics but was offered a position as Judge of the Illinois Tenth Circuit Court during his first year in office. He accepted the offer and served on the bench for several years. However, it wasn't long before he was setting his sights even higher, this time as a Republican candidate for the United States Congress, and he handily won the election in 1857.

The Judge fondly recalled proudly campaigning for his father during his bid for the U.S. Congress when he was 12. Accompanying his father to many of his stump speeches, he passed out hundreds of posters emblazoned with his father's name. Their family made many such sacrifices over the years so that his father could finally achieve such a position of honor. After the election, they celebrated the Congressman's victory and his prestigious journey from humble Illinois lawyer to ranking member of the House. However, the Congressman would now be gone more than ever, working in Washington D.C. with his fellow members of Congress for the next six years until 1863.

His absence coincided with a crucial time when the Judge, like Willie, was transitioning from a boy to a young man. The Judge missed his father terribly, as did his mother and younger siblings, John and Paulina. So much of the responsibility of the home fell squarely on his mother's shoulders, and she relied on her eldest son to help her take care of his siblings when their father was away. It was also a pivotal time in American history. Lincoln had been elected to the presidency amid great controversy, with the threat of civil war on the horizon in 1861. Lincoln and the Congressman had been close friends for several years through their mutual political connections in Illinois.

The Congressman and the President became close allies on many issues involving the looming war. He was even said to have been in secret meetings with President Lincoln drafting a proposal designed to avoid the war. On February 8, 1861, the Congressman unveiled the substance of his proposal and gave an address to the House suggesting a compromise on the issues at stake. The Congressman was immediately criticized by many of his fellow colleagues—and his constituents back home in Illinois—because his proposal allowed slavery to continue in certain states under certain conditions.

Opinions were divided. Arguments were heated. And neither side of the issue was willing to back down. In the end, his proposal was defeated, and no amount of debate and discussion could stop the first guns from firing at Fort Sumter on April 12, 1861, plunging the entire nation into the Civil War.

In a desperate effort to look out for his son, shortly after the war broke out Congressman Kellogg secured an appointment for him to the United States Military Academy at West Point in New York. Like many young men inspired by the dramatic events surrounding the Civil War, Cadet Kellogg was at first excited about his prospects at the prestigious school alongside his fellow cadets. But his enthusiasm soon waned, revealing that perhaps it was the influence of his father (and his efforts to please him) that had driven his desire to serve in the military.

Disciplinary issues started popping up on Cadet Kellogg's record. The boy's youthful, rebellious nature had difficulty following the strict rules of the academy. His superiors quickly filled several pages of carefully handwritten notations of his offenses. The violations were not major, but there were a lot of them. He was cited for not carrying his hands in the proper position while marching to dinner and laughing while standing at attention in the ranks. The officers watched him like a hawk, perhaps hoping the Congressman's privileged son might fail. Cadet Kellogg did not disappoint.

By May 1862 he was discharged as a "casualty," as the Academy put it, for excessive demerits. Embarrassed by his son's dismissal, Congressman Kellogg stepped in once again by using his influence to secure a second chance, and Cadet Kellogg was readmitted to the Academy two months later in July 1862. However, he was soon buried in demerits again. He was forced to march for hours before the barracks with his musket for all to see as punishment for his alleged worst offense—assaulting a Sentinel—which had led to his court martial.

Even so, his father was always on his side and doggedly loyal in supporting him. He wondered if he had been that kind of father to his children, now 1,600 miles away in Toronto? He reached again into his memory box on the shelf and pulled out a yellow and tattered handwritten letter his father had written him while at the Academy in January 1863. He smiled as he read it:

Washington
January 18, 1863

My Dear Son,

I suppose you know the result of the Court Martial. In your case, it is a reprimand— confined to the plain until next September and march before the barracks with a musket every Saturday afternoon until next June. This is more than was inflicted on any other cadet. It is assumed that the reason for that is that you assaulted a sentinel. I saw General Hallask, but he refused to change it. (By the way, I think he is a poor stick.) I did not go to the Secretary of War or President but concluded that about the time I have, I would try and get the sentence modified or revoked. I don't know as I can do it but will try. Colonel Ruggles speaks highly of your ability and says that you can occupy any place in your class that you wish. I think the members of the court thought they have dealt lightly with all. My advice is to submit cheerfully and fix your mind firmly on graduating with credit. I know you can.

Your sister and John have both been here to see us and have left for school. John is doing well, I think, and for the first time in his life is interested and trying to learn. Your sister is doing well and says she will write you. I will send their pictures to you.

There is little of interest here. Everybody is despponding, but I hope and believe that all will yet be well, and the government saved from destruction.

Don't fail to write me on receipt of this.

Your father

By the start of 1864, the War still had another year to grind on. Regrettably, by February 1864 the Academy had enough of

Cadet Kellogg. Notwithstanding his father's position, he was discharged for the final time, earning a place on the official West Point Register of Cadet Casualties for excessive demerits. His offenses totaled 110 by that point, all meticulously hand-recorded in beautiful script by his superior officers in the annals of West Point.

Looking back, the Judge knew that he'd had a rough go controlling his youthful rebellious tendencies at the Academy. Notwithstanding the embarrassment of his final dismissal, his father received him back in Peoria like the Prodigal Son, encouraging him to join his law practice and study to become a lawyer.

The Judge knew he had let his father down, so he readily agreed to give it a try. Perhaps his independent personality would find the law a better fit than the rigid structure of the military. He reasoned that he could work the hours he wanted and choose the cases he wanted to take on.

A year later, the Civil War mercifully came to an end in the spring of 1865. It left in its wake over 600,000 dead and many cities in complete ruin. The period that followed, later known as Reconstruction, would prove to be equally long and bitter.

The Congressman opted not to seek re-election after the war and instead returned home to Illinois to be with his family and work in his law practice full time. The Judge was now 20 years of age and hoped to pass the bar exam soon. With his father's name to build on, he anticipated a successful career as an attorney in Peoria while the country attempted to heal its wounds.

President Lincoln was grateful to Congressman Kellogg for his support during the war and offered him the position of U.S. Minister to Guatemala. But the Congressman was tired of being away from home. Feeling his family needed him, he respectfully declined. Lincoln then offered to appoint him Chief Justice of the Supreme Court of the Nebraska Territory, which included Nebraska, most of Wyoming and Montana, and parts of Colorado and North and South Dakota. While this would require some travel by train when court was in session, most of his work could be done from his law office in Peoria where he could continue to mentor his son's emerging law practice.

He agreed and President Lincoln nominated him for the position in early 1865, but he still had to be confirmed by the United States Senate. While his nomination was pending, President Lincoln invited the Congressman to dinner at the White House on April 1, 1865. After dining on pheasant, they each enjoyed a fine Cuban cigar and a sniffer of brandy on the small porch outside the President's private quarters.

The cherry trees on the lawn were in full bloom as the

sun sank below the horizon. The President leaned in and said, "William, I know you will be confirmed. I want to see Nebraska become a state, not just a territory, mind you. Use all your influence and skills to help make that happen once you are confirmed. Understood?"

The Congressman nodded and said, "Mr. President, you have my word on it."

But two weeks later on the evening April 14, 1865, President Lincoln was assassinated by John Wilkes Booth in Washington, D.C. while attending a play with Mrs. Lincoln at Ford's Theater. He died the next morning. The nation mourned and expressed their collective grief over the shocking turn of events. It was a loss for the country and a very personal loss for the Congressman.

The Congressman's nomination was confirmed soon after, and on May 15, 1865, President Andrew Johnson swore him in. As the Congressman took the oath, his thoughts were with his now departed friend and the last words he spoke to him at the White House. He was determined to do all he could to move Nebraska toward statehood as the President wanted.

Meanwhile, his wife was busy raising twin girls nicknamed Lulu and Lud. The Judge, now in his early twenties, loved his much younger sisters and often took on the role of their father when the Congressman was out of town on official business in Nebraska. In fact, the little girls were sometimes mistaken as his own children, such was the age gap between them. The Judge didn't mind, as he hoped to have children of his own one day and considered this good practice.

During his father's time as Chief Judge of the territory from 1865 to 1867, he was busy lobbying for Nebraska to be admitted into the United States. Finally, just as his term was expiring, Nebraska was admitted as the 37th state. When the Congressman returned fulltime to Peoria in 1867, President Johnson rewarded him for his service by appointing him Collector of Internal Revenue for the Peoria District, a position he held from 1867 to 1869 while he continued his law practice in partnership with his son.

For the next five years the pair seemed inseparable, as father taught son the intricacies of the practice of law. The Judge's memories about this time with his father and his evolution to young adulthood seemed more like a blur than the many years they covered. When he lost his father to a sudden illness a few days before Christmas in 1872, the Judge realized just how quickly the years had passed by. At 28 years of age, the Judge stood stoically at the graveside as his father was laid to rest in Springdale Cemetery in Peoria. He put his arm around his grieving mother and sisters and felt the full weight of the family's future coming firmly to rest on his shoulders. Could he handle it? He had to do so; he had no choice.

⸱⊷═◉ ◉═⊶⸱

LEADVILLE, COLORADO 1891

Sitting in his office in Leadville, the tin memory box in his lap, the Judge wrestled with his nagging fear of disappointing the people he loved. Things had not improved since his father's death. He was so tired and burdened by the fact that he could never seem to get ahead. The Judge had failed his own expectations when the silver mining went belly up. He had failed his late wife. And he had failed his children, not being able to care for them in Leadville. He no longer had the refuge of his family. His wife was dead, as was their youngest son. His three living children were scattered to the winds. The family home was empty. He felt old, sick, and defeated.

Familiar depression settled on him like a black cloud as he folded his father's letter and Abbie's telegram into the box and replaced it on the shelf. His work no longer sufficiently distracted him from his emotions. So he did what he always did at the end of a workday—routinely packing his satchel with some work papers he would take home to read later as he began the lonely walk home.

As he closed the door to his office, he heard a voice in his heart.

"Listen to me, dear..." Abbie's voice was strong. "You made it through another day. And remember—our precious Abbie is having a baby, and that baby is going to love and need his grandfather. You focus on the future and don't worry about the past."

As the Judge locked the door, his wife's loving words brought a small smile to his lips. With that fleeting encouragement in mind, he continued his walk home to spend another long night alone.

TORONTO, FALL 1891

For the first few months of Abbie's pregnancy, Pauline second-guessed her decision to move away from Toronto back to Peoria. She did not want to be so far away from her sister and the new baby. Although she did not necessarily feel any maternal desire to have children of her own, she envied the opportunity to be there for Abbie.

Meanwhile, Abbie tried to stay occupied in the early days of her pregnancy, cleaning house and setting up the nursery for the new baby. William left early every morning for the office and worked late. The young couple often had only the late evenings to catch up, reminisce about their time together thus far, and dream about the future. Abbie loved it when William would recall how they met, fell in love, and got married. He was a natural storyteller, and her favorite story was about their honeymoon.

A month before their wedding in October 1890, a large brown envelope had arrived at William's office from the Edison Electric Light Company in New York. More company business, he thought, and more work he didn't have time to do. William tossed the unopened envelope on the corner of his desk until he could find time later to get to it. He was in a hurry. He was supposed to meet with Abbie and the Presbyterian preacher at 3:00 that Friday afternoon to discuss their wedding plans. So he closed the door to his office and hurried off to meet his future bride.

When he returned to the office Monday morning, he instinctively started digging through his pile of work to prioritize the week ahead. He had to be efficient. Time was precious, and he had very little of it. He picked up Friday's brown envelope, slit it open with his pocketknife, and pulled out the packet of papers. But to his surprise they were not the engineering drawings he expected. The top sheet was a handwritten letter on company stationery, which read:

My Dear William,

We were so pleased to have received your most kind invitation to attend your wedding in November.

Regrettably, I must advise that Mrs. Edison and I will be unable to make the trip to Toronto due to prior commitments. But, having met your Abbie on my last trip out to the hinder-land, I have no reason to doubt that you have made a superb choice and that the two of you will be very happy together. Please accept our warmest congratulations.

It's difficult to believe it has been nearly 10 years now since you joined the company. During this time, you have repeatedly proven yourself not only a superb electrical engineer and dedicated employee, but also you have helped lead our company's expansion in an admirable fashion.

I am so grateful. You have become so much more than just an employee. We consider you more like family, my dear young friend. I know you have a very bright future.

Please accept the enclosed as my way of thanking you for all you have done. Mina and I wish you and Abbie the very best for your new future together. I advise you to leave your work behind, as it will still be there upon your return. Go and

enjoy your honeymoon with Abbie with my bless-
ing. I hope you like what I have dreamed up for
the two of you.

Your friend,
Thomas A. Edison

William was stunned as he looked at the next sheet in the packet entitled "Scotland Itinerary for Mr. & Mrs. William E. Davis November 30, 1890 – January 5, 1891." William was speechless. As his eyes raced down the page, he realized that Mr. Edison was gifting them a fully paid honeymoon trip to Scotland.

"Oh my," he thought. "Is this is really happening?"

In the thick envelope were two first-class roundtrip tickets to Scotland on the steamship *SS Abyssinia*. The voyage over the Atlantic would take six days from Toronto to Port Glasgow, Scotland, which he realized was a very fast journey. Prior to modern screw propulsion steamers, a trip overseas would take 15 days with older paddle-wheeled steamers. Today's innovations had more than cut that time in half. He dug deeper into the packet of papers. In addition to detailed arrangements for train, hotel, and carriage services across Scotland, there was a nice stipend included for expenses.

He could not wait to tell Abbie. She would be thrilled. He rushed out of the office and hurried to Grandpa Jesse's house to tell her the news. They had both been wanting to travel, and this was their chance, thanks to the generosity and friendship of Mr. Edison. They could never afford such a trip on their own.

As William burst through the front door he proclaimed, "Come here, Abbie darling. You are not going to believe this." He handed her the letter, and she quickly read it.

"How can this be?" she cried. She knew it was real when he showed her the steamship tickets.

"William, I love you so much," she exclaimed, throwing her arms around him. "I can't wait to spend the rest of my life with you!"

Abbie knew from the first time she met Mr. Edison how much he really cared for William. He treated William more like a son than an employee. Sometimes she wondered if perhaps Mr. Edison saw a younger version of himself in William. Whatever the reason behind his generosity, she was so grateful. She and William talked long into the night planning and dreaming about their trip.

"William," Abbie asked, "is there any way we can visit Fingal's Cave on the Isle of Staffa?"

"What is Fingal's Cave? And where did you hear of it? It's not on the itinerary," William replied.

She quickly told him how she had learned about the mysterious cave in Miss Godfrey's English class at Wolfe Hall as part of her reading assignment about the Scottish poet James McPherson. He had written a Gaelic poem about the cave. In the poem, there was a mythological Irish giant named Fionn mac Cumhaill, who had built the causeway between Ireland and Scotland. The unusual cave was supposedly a hiding place for the heroic giant as he dealt with his enemies who opposed the causeway.

Abbie recalled the sketch in her textbook of the cave that had always intrigued her. She would give anything for the chance to see Fingal's Cave in real life.

"Can we go? Please, please, please?" she begged, reverting to more of the giddy teenager she was than a mature soon-to-be-married woman.

He never could resist Abbie's charms. "Sweetheart, if it means that much to you, we will go see this Fingal's Cave or drown trying," he laughed.

William, true to his word, made it happen. And it turned out to be the very best part of their trip.

⊶⊷

One year later as their first wedding anniversary approached, Abbie had something very special in mind for William—something she had been secretly working on for many months.

A few months earlier while William was at work, she had

come across the sketch of Fingal's Cave that she'd started when they were in Scotland. She set it next to her easel, stretched a new canvas, and began a more detailed drawing of the elusive cave they both had so enjoyed.

Slowly, she transformed the rough sketch into a beautiful oil painting of towering cliffs, crashing waves, and out-of-this-world rugged hexagon columns rising from the sea on the sides of the dark cave. With a feathery stroke she added a small ship in the distance and two lone figures atop the cliffs, peering at the dark sea's horizon.

Each evening before William returned from work, she removed the canvas from her easel, covered it with a sheet, and hid it in a closet. After several months, she was satisfied and signed the lower right corner of the canvas: *Abbie Kellogg - November 27, 1890.* Their wedding day. In the left corner she wrote *Fingal's Cave – Staffa.*

On November 27, 1891, the young couple went out to one of Toronto's top restaurants to celebrate their first anniversary as husband and wife. Money was tight, but this was a special night and they splurged. After they got home, Abbie sat William down on the side of the bed and told him to close his eyes and promise not to peek. As he dutifully obeyed, she retrieved the finished painting hidden in the closet and held it in front of him.

"This is for you, my love. Open your eyes!'" she declared.

His mouth fell open in surprise. "Abbie! When did you ever find the time to do this?"

She smiled and said, "Well, with our first child on the way and you gone all the time, I had to have *something* to keep me occupied."

William leaned the painting against a nearby chair as they laughed and wrapped their arms around each other.

The next morning after breakfast, William asked, "Where shall we hang our new masterpiece?"

"Anywhere you like, Mr. Davis. I am just the artist," Abbie said.

"Well, I think it needs to go in a place of honor over the fireplace mantel," William replied. "It will always remind us of our honeymoon."

She agreed, and after William fetched a hammer and nail, up it went at the center of their home. The painting would always remain a centerpiece of their home for the rest of their lives—wherever they might be and however long or short the rest of their lives might prove to be.

⊷═◎═⊶

As the months flew by and the birth of their child grew closer, William's work only seemed to stack up all around him. He could never seem to catch up. Ever since the fateful day he helped a pretty young lady retrieve her apples on the streets of Toronto, everything had been going William's way. Toronto was booming, and the city held so many opportunities for innovative engineers like William. The Toronto Incandescent Electric Light Company held the Canadian rights to Edison's patents and William worked closely with them to convert the city's extensive railway system. Together, they supplied the electric power for the long-held dream of transforming Toronto's horse-drawn transit system into electrified rails.

In its last year of use, the old, horse-powered railway in Toronto carried 55,000 passengers using 264 horsecars, 99 buses, 100 sleighs and 1,372 horses. The railway had about 80 miles of track and 68 miles of routes. However, under William's supervision, the city began electrifying its horse-drawn tracks using Edison's technology. Toronto leaders wanted to provide service to the city and also to the burgeoning suburban population outside the city limits and beyond.

The complicated project was all William's baby, and he poured himself into his work with great enthusiasm. Many people often commented about his gift for friendship with clients, suppliers, and colleagues. His easy-going approach made working with his important clientele something he managed with ease, although he was consequently inundated with work that was entrusted to him.

He was now barely 30 years old, but William's reputation in the electric power industry was growing by leaps and bounds. It was quite an adventure for a young man, but he had the same work ethic he had first learned from his father. As successful as William was, he never forgot his working-class roots and the blue-collar neighborhood he grew up in in Fall River, Massachusetts. William also had a rugged simplicity about him that others took note of. He could get along with the highest executives with the same easy demeanor as he did common laborers. His competence in his field and natural intelligence, paired with a sparkling wit, drew others to him and put them at ease.

William had witnessed the rapport he'd seen his father display with his customers, whether working part-time carpentry or mechanic jobs or delivering produce from his farm into town on market day. William's father put the best of himself into every job, and he always prioritized the people over everything else. If a man can be trusted, his father had told him as a young boy, that man will never be short on work. William never forgot that lesson, and he emulated his father in many ways.

Between endless meetings, William enjoyed a good joke

with his colleagues and often drew them in with a story or two that kept them entertained in the middle of the workday. His lightning-fast repartee had his coworkers and clients in fits of laughter. He was just a lot of fun, as Abbie and many others could attest.

William also had a way with verse and was a bit of an amateur poet, something unexpected of the typical engineer. He delighted friends and family with witty original poems about politics, work, and even the more serious issues of life. Abbie liked to say her husband was a bit of a renaissance man for his time. She honestly enjoyed everything about William. He almost always woke up happy in the mornings and moved about with a cheery smile on his face while getting ready for work.

Abbie learned she could count on her husband's consistency of character, one of the things that she'd fallen in love with early on. Above all, Abbie knew he would be a good father when their child arrived in May, and that time was rapidly approaching.

William worked day and night during the spring as Abbie's belly grew larger with their first child. His job was stressful and full of difficult work, but it was also rewarding. He could finally afford a growing family and looked forward to not just one, but a house-full of children one day with his Abbie. Life was ripe with wonder and unlimited opportunity for William and Abbie.

⊷⊜ ⊜⊶

LEADVILLE, COLORADO 1892

As he was sworn in as the District Attorney in Leadville on New Year's Day 1892, the Judge found himself unceremoniously back where he'd started. The path that had led to this election as District Attorney again made his career and life appear to be going in circles.

The year after his wife died, the Judge had seized the opportunity to take a position as the Judge of the new Criminal Court for the Fifth Judicial District of Colorado. No doubt, his carefully honed political connections helped him land the appointment by Colorado's new governor, Alvah Adams. He'd had had the foresight to support Adams in the last election. Discerning the right horse to back was a skill he had learned from his father, the politician. As the Honorable Judge Kellogg, he wore a title that brought him even greater respect and notoriety within the Leadville community and beyond.

The Judge had served on the bench faithfully and with distinction, and in his private thoughts, he even began to imagine all the ways this position might someday lead to a higher office. Perhaps he would serve in the Colorado legislature or even the United States Congress like his father. But in 1891 the political winds changed, and the legislature chose to abolish the Fifth Judicial District Criminal Court over which he presided. He was out of a job, leaving him devastated and bereft.

He was still financially supporting Pauline in Peoria and Willie in Michigan, while also looking after his mother and sisters. Too many people depended on him. The Judge had to find work. In September that year he reluctantly went back to what he knew best but no longer enjoyed: practicing law. He briefly partnered with another local attorney named Frank E. Purple to form a new law firm entitled Kellogg & Purple. But that partnership did not last long. The Judge foresaw that trying to re-enter the private practice of law was going to be slow and difficult, so he began looking at other options, including running again for District Attorney. If he couldn't be a judge any longer, being a District Attorney with a steady salary beat trying to restart a law practice in the middle of a depression caused by the silver crash.

It humbled him greatly to run in the next election for his old position of District Attorney. Well-liked and respected, he was re-elected District Attorney of Fifth Judicial District for the second time a few months later on November 8, 1891. He had his old job back and at least he would have a steady job to meet his obligations.

The Judge carried these burdens alone for the most part, although he did on occasion share some of his growing despair with his sister Lou. On January 14, 1892, he wrote her a letter on his defunct law firm stationery about the seemingly never-ending, circular tedium of his life.

KELLOGG & PURPLE
Attorneys
Leadville, Colorado

January 14ᵗʰ, 1892

My Dear Lou,

I am a little late in acknowledging your kind remembrance of Dec 25ᵗʰ but with my rheumatics, and taking hold of the new office, I have been pretty busy. I received a nice letter the other day from Em. They were all well, and she seemed to be quite happy with her "hubby" and the baby. I shall write to her today. Letters from Wissie assure me that the tribe in that end of the world are getting along quite nicely.

I should have liked very much to have visited with you all on Christmas Day, but at that time and for a week prior, I was confined to my room. And besides, money was too scarce with me for a trip of that kind. I still live in hope, however, that I may sometime be able to take the trip. I hope Pauline is not too mad at me to write. It has been a long time since I heard from her. Did she receive the money I sent for this month? She has not acknowledged its receipt. I sent it about the 28th or 29th of December.

We are having a bitter cold winter—plenty of snow and elegant sleighing—though I haven't had a sleigh ride this winter. Am getting worked into my old trade slowly, though there is not much to do just now.

Give my love to Mother and Pauline, not forgetting Louisa.

Brother Bill

He'd fallen out with Pauline by that time. Her letters to him from Peoria, and his to her, came fewer and far between.

Willie likewise continued to flounder aimlessly during the first few months of military school in Michigan. Both kids still seemed angry at him. Abbie, however, was the one bright spot in the Judge's life. She seemed so happy with William in Toronto. His spirits brightened as he shared with Lou his happiness that Abbie would give birth to her first child, and his first grandchild, at any moment. On April 11, 1892, he wrote Lou again:

KELLOGG & PURPLE
Attorneys
Leadville, Colorado

April 11ᵗʰ, 1892

My Dear Lou,

We are having a cold, muddy spring, if this can be called spring. Business is dull, and everything is quiet here. I am reconciled to the idea of being Grandpa, because I suppose I have to stand it.

I hope the young one is getting along alright. She writes cheerfully and as though she was very happy. Willie is spending his vacation with a friend in Detroit and was feeling quite grand when I heard

from him last. A Mr. Clark and family of whom
Pauline speaks in her last letter was here passing
through. Judge Hull told me he met them at the
depot, but I did not see them.

There is nothing of interest transpiring here.

Brother Bill

The benign close to his short letter later betrayed him, but he was unaware then of all of that was about to change in only a few weeks' time. Something was about to occur that would send his whole world into yet another tailspin.

TORONTO, CANADA 1892

By late April of 1892, Abbie busied herself making final preparations for their new baby, anxiously counting down the remaining weeks. How she longed for her mother's comforting presence with each passing day. There were so many questions she would ask her mother, if only she were here. What had her mother done to get ready for her first child? Was she as anxious and happy as Abbie?

She knew William would be there for her, holding her hand and encouraging her. He'd told her so over and over, trying to ease her angst. Nevertheless, Abbie could not help but remember her mom's suffering in childbirth. Like flies, she tried to shoo those negative thoughts away whenever they crept into her mind. What she had to do was keep telling herself that this time was different, and everything would go just fine.

After all, she felt good and hadn't Doctor Sanford just been by a few days ago to check up on her? She and William had grinned from ear to ear when he packed away his stethoscope and pronounced her "fit as a fiddle." The doctor had noted her blood pressure was a little high, but it was nothing to be worried about, he assured them. It was springtime, the season of renewal, and she and William could not wait to hold their first child in their arms.

Abbie was cooking breakfast a few weeks later the morning of May 20 when she felt the first contractions. She calmly interrupted William's morning coffee, saying, "William, I believe it is time."

He nearly spilled his coffee and quickly forgot all that he was supposed to do, although he and Abbie had rehearsed the list many times. Throwing his arms around his wife in an embrace, he then remembered his first job was to summon the midwife. They'd already made plans for her to come to the house whenever Abbie's labor started, and William scurried off to fetch her.

They'd both met the midwife weeks earlier and liked her immensely. Doctor Sanford had given his approval as well. While Abbie felt that the doctor should also be there just in case, he and William had reassured her that, if needed, he could get there quick enough.

When William returned with the midwife, his warm and confident smile helped put Abbie at ease, reminding her that everything was going to go perfectly. He would send for the doctor immediately if there were any problems.

It was a hard labor lasting almost 24 hours. At 5:00 on the morning of May 21, Abbie gave birth to a beautiful baby boy. The midwife laid the baby next to her as William held her hand.

"See, Abbie?" William said softly. "Everything is fine, just as I promised."

"Hello, Leonard Ellsworth Davis," she announced as she held her child. "Welcome to the world, my little boy." His first name was in honor of her brother as they had discussed, and "Ellsworth" was Abbie's choice to honor her husband. It was a strong name, she thought, perfect for the healthy infant snuggling against her.

Abbie dozed off, then she and William took turns holding the newborn for most of the morning. They were so proud of the bundle of joy in their arms. Neither one had ever felt anything like this before. This perfect baby was all theirs, and they had created this tiny human being through their love for each other. William beamed, thinking he could not wait to do this again. He would savor the memories of that peaceful first morning together for years afterwards, just him, Abbie, and Leonard.

⊰⊱●○●⊰⊱

"What's happening to me?" Abbie asked, wild-eyed with anxiety. It was noon and Abbie's heartrate was accelerating. "This isn't right, something's wrong," she insisted.

No, it wasn't right, and yes something was wrong, William agreed as did the midwife. He left Abbie with her and hurried off to get Doctor Sanford. The doctor rushed over, took one look at Abbie and said, "We've got to get her to the hospital."

They all piled into the doctor's carriage, William holding the baby with one arm and the other holding Abbie, who had collapsed on his shoulder. Within twenty minutes they were at St. Michael's Hospital in Toronto.

The nurses immediately took Abbie to a room, and they placed Leonard in a bassinet by her bed. The doctor on call took samples of Abbie's blood and urine, which were hustled off by a nurse into the inner recesses of the hospital. Then the long wait for the results began.

After an hour passed, Abbie began moaning and crying out incoherently, first for William, then for her baby. She was sweating, then shivering, thrashing about in the bed. William

122

pointed out to the nurse how his wife's breath was ragged and quick. He was so scared. He was no doctor, but William feared she was slipping further away with each passing hour.

Finally, Doctor Sanford entered the room holding some paperwork from the lab. "Puerperal pre-eclampsia," he said.

"What? What's that?" William demanded. "Doc, will she be alright? Just please tell me she will…please!" he pleaded.

"William, I will be honest with you. It doesn't look good. This is a rare condition that sometimes occurs when the mother has excessive protein in her urine and high blood pressure," he explained to an unhearing, unfeeling William. He was numb. Speechless. He tried to focus on what the doctor was saying about how quickly this disease could be triggered after birth. It was rare, but it happened.

"But she was absolutely fine this morning," William protested. "I told her everything would be okay. I promised her that, you see? Please, dear God, help us…" But his words were drowned out by the flurry of activity around Abbie from several nurses who were beginning to appear panicked and distraught themselves.

Less than six hours after the birth of Leonard, Abbie succumbed to unforeseen complications from childbirth. The hospital staff had tried valiantly all afternoon and evening to get her runaway blood pressure and heartrate down, but they were unsuccessful.

"Why couldn't you help her?" William cried. "What should I have…" His voice trailed off.

"Son, there wasn't a thing you or I could do. After this disease takes hold of a young mother, it's so hard to stop. I've seen it too many times," Doctor Sanford lamented, placing a hand on William's shoulder. "I'm so sorry. We did all we could, but it just wasn't meant to be." He paused. "Didn't you say Abbie's mother died giving birth as well?"

William nodded.

"We think more and more that the pre-eclampsia condition is often passed down from mother to child. That could explain why this happened. I guess it's like lightning striking twice," he muttered.

William sat down on the chair next to the hospital bed, peering at his wife's lifeless body. He reached out and took her limp, cold hand, unwilling to accept the reality. A few feet away, Leonard was cooing in his bassinet as a nurse made sure he was warm and fed.

William could no longer contain his tears. He wept like he had never done before. The nurses tried to console him, but nothing seemed to help.

Finally, Grandpa Jesse and Annie arrived. They suggested to William that he and the baby come home with them for a few days as they figured out what to do. William, in a daze, reluctantly agreed. He asked for one more moment alone with Abbie before leaving, and Jesse and Annie took the baby outside into the hallway.

Through bloodshot eyes, William looked down at Abbie's body. "I am so sorry, my sweet Abbie," he said, tears streaming down his face as leaned over and placed a tender kiss on her cool forehead. He could say nothing else. Then he walked out of the room and joined Grandpa Jesse, Annie, and his son.

Married less than two years, William was heartbroken. Abbie was his first love, and as far as William was concerned, would remain his only love. He endured the burden of planning his young wife's funeral and laid her to rest four days later on May 25 in Mount Pleasant Cemetery in Toronto. A few weeks later, William purchased a headstone that simply read:

ABBIE
BELOVED WIFE OF
W.E. DAVIS
DIED MAY 21ST, 1892
18 YEARS, SIX MONTHS, 21 DAYS

None of William's family could travel from Massachusetts for the funeral, but Pauline and Willie were there, accompanied by their Aunt Lou and Grandma Lucinda from Peoria. Their father, the Judge, was too sickly and frail to make the long journey from Leadville.

Pauline understood why her father could not come, but she was angry all the same. As she tossed a pale pink rose into the grave of her sister, she made a solemn vow. She wanted no part of marriage or children of her own. After losing her mother, her baby brother, and now Abbie, Pauline realized the possibility of losing someone else was more than she could bear. It was too painful to say goodbye to someone you loved, so she decided once and for all that she would be alone the rest of her life rather than risk another heartache.

After the funeral, the reality of William's situation began to sink in while he stayed at Grandpa Jesse's home. He was a single parent with a newborn son living in someone else's house. But William couldn't take care of a newborn baby by himself, something he knew little about how to do. He had to get back to work.

While he greatly appreciated Grandpa Jesse and Annie's help, he knew it was an imposition and not a long-term solution. Grandpa Jesse was now 60 years of age, and Annie was approaching 50. They had their hands full raising their own children. Raising their great-grandchild was out of the question. The Judge was no help. He was in poor health and could barely take care of himself in Leadville. William's own parents were also getting on in years, plus they were too far away.

His only option, William concluded, was his older sister back in Fall River. Lulietta Davis Read (1860-1910) had experienced her own share of tragedy at a young age, having lost her husband, Fredrick M. Read, two years before Abbie's death. Lulie was a 30-year-old widow with two children, Fred Jr. age 12 and Charlotte (nicknamed Lottie) age 10.

William wrote to Lulie and asked her for the greatest favor any parent can ask. Would she be willing to take Leonard into her family and raise him as her own? It was an excruciating choice. Yet in his heart, he knew it would be the best for everyone. Lulie was struggling financially, and he could help support her if she were willing to take in Leonard. Next to Abbie, he believed Lulie would be the best substitute he could hope for. She was a young, good person who knew how to take care of a child, he reasoned. William made it clear in his letter how much he appreciated his sister and that he would send regular financial payments to help with the extra expenses. After reading it over one more time, he mailed the letter and awaited her answer.

⊷⊜ ⊜⊶

LEADVILLE, COLORADO 1892

The Judge received news of Abbie's death by telegram. He spoke to no one for three days afterward. He did not go into the office. And he did not answer the door at home. Life had dealt him another devastating blow. First his wife, then his son, now his daughter—all taken in childbirth. He was despondent and angry at the twisted finger of fate.

The joy he'd been anticipating in becoming a grandfather was gone in an instant. Although he'd wanted to attend the funeral, he did not feel his worn-out body could possibly make such a long and hurried trip. Besides, he wasn't sure he could even afford it. After a few weeks, he finally wrote his sister Lou lamenting his daughter's surprising death.

> *Office of Wm. Kellogg*
> *Leadville, Colorado*
> *June 7, 1892*
>
> *My Dear Lou,*
>
> *I rec'd your kind letter a day or two ago. Yes, Abbie's death was a surprise and a blow to me, but I have about come to think that I am a special mark for unpleasant things and take them now as much as a matter of course as I can.*

I am thinking of sending Willie up to your country, if you and Ma think best, and if you could make room for him during his vacations. I rec'd from Pauline a catalogue of a Tacoma School, and she said she would find out about one at Seattle. Do you know anything about them or which is best? Willie's school is out early in July, and I must then send him somewhere. I don't want him here, and if you are all agreeable, I will have him go direct to Tacoma either by the Canadian Pacific or U.P., whichever is the cheapest. So let me know what you think of the matter. The school matter can be decided upon later.

Love to all. Write soon.

Bro Bill

I sent money to Pauline by Ex. for this month on the 21st of last, but cannot hear whether it was rec'd or not, was it?

The Judge's rheumatism was slowly ebbing away his life. He struggled each day just to get out of bed and make himself a cup of coffee. Everything he loved, it seemed, had been taken from him. Pauline and Willie barely acknowledged him,

129

although he continued to send them money and fatherly advice in his letters. His only real family was now his sister Lou. They continued to write each other fairly often in the year following Abbie's death. He made one futile trip to New Mexico in late 1892 seeking treatment for his illness, but only 15 months after Abbie's death, the Judge died alone in Leadville on August 12, 1893, just shy of his 49th birthday.

⊷⊷⊷

FALL RIVER, MASSACHUSETTS 1892

After reading her brother's letter, Lulie visited with Fred and Lottie about taking Leonard into their family. Lulie told them in no uncertain terms that it would require all three of them to raise a baby in their home. Were they ready for the responsibility? To her surprise Lottie was ecstatic to have a newborn baby brother. Fred was less enthusiastic, but he agreed he'd do his best to help out.

After hearing from his sister, William boarded a train with tiny Leonard in his arms for the long journey from Toronto to Massachusetts. The passengers on the train were surprised to see a single man caring for a newborn, especially with the tender love he openly displayed. William solemnly stared out the train window as the scenery flew by in a blur, consumed by thoughts of his predicament. Occasionally, he would look down at the sleeping baby next to him and think, "I hope I can do this."

Soon he arrived at the station in Fall River and took a carriage to Lulie's modest home in a quiet part of town. William took a deep breath, knocked on the front door, and waited for his sister to answer. When Lulie opened the door she saw her brother, gaunt with grief, holding a tiny infant who was cooing and playfully reaching up to grasp his father's chin. Lulie looked to William for permission as she slowly scooped the bundle out from the crook of her brother's arm and nestled her face into the baby's cheek. Leonard fastened a firm grip around Lulie's finger and smiled, completely unaware of the seriousness of the moment.

"Come in, William!" she cried, holding Leonard with one arm and holding the door with the other. "Come in this house!"

William smiled as Fred and Lottie ran to their mother to inspect the little boy she was holding.

"Can we really keep him, Mother?" Lottie asked innocently.

"Yes, dear. This is Leonard—he's going to be your new baby brother."

Even as she spoke those words, William grimaced and his gut felt as if it were turning over. He spent a sleepless night at

Lulie's and left early the next morning. He was afraid that if he stayed any longer, he might change his mind. The pain was unbearable on top of what he had already suffered in losing Abbie.

"Abbie, darling," he whispered repeatedly into the night as he tossed and turned in his sister's guest bedroom, "please forgive me. Please tell me this is the right thing to do." He had no choice, but the guilt was overwhelming.

⋗═◉ ◉═⋖

TORONTO 1892

On the long train ride back to Toronto, William replayed his decision over and over in his mind. Why was something that was for the best making him feel so guilty and lost? As the days, weeks, and months crawled by, he poured himself into his work. But his mood continued to deteriorate. He was no longer the optimistic person he was only a few months before. Everything had changed for the worse. Would it ever get any better? He wondered.

One Friday in September William was having lunch with another Edison employee at the George Street Diner a few blocks from the office. William was his usual somber self as he aimlessly stirred his bowl of soup.

"William, how are you doing?" Percy asked him. Percival Gallon (1869-1915) was a construction foreman who had worked closely with William for several years. He was seven years younger than William and they weren't close friends, but William liked him and thought he was a hard worker.

"Oh, I'm doing alright, I guess," William replied absent-mindedly.

"Well, you sure don't act like it," Percy muttered. "Look, I know you have been through a rough patch, and I feel for you. What are you doing to get out of the house and have some fun?"

William was uncomfortable with the question. He was just working and going home to an empty house and told Percy as much.

"Hey," Percy replied, "why don't you come with me to my parents' ranch this weekend? It will give you something to do other than work. They live up near Lindsay, about three hours by train from here."

"Oh, I don't know..." William began.

"Oh, come on, William," Percy interrupted. "Let's get out of here."

Percy did make him laugh from time to time, so William broke a faint smile and said, "Oh, alright. Maybe it will do me some good. Thanks for the invitation."

That Friday morning, they boarded the train heading for
the town of Lindsay near Sturgeon Lake. Percy's father was
the sheriff of Victoria County and quite a character. He met
them at the train station, and they rode out to the ranch in his
carriage. As soon as they arrived at the ranch house, Sheriff
Gallon quickly made plans for the afternoon.

"Come on, boys, let's go shoot some grouse," he said. "Mrs.
Gallon will make us up some dinner while we're gone. If we're
lucky it will be grouse!"

William had never been hunting for grouse before, but
they did well and brought six back home. Percy's mother,
Mary, started preparing the birds for dinner.

That evening William and Percy sat down to a wonderful
meal with the Gallons and two of their youngest children who
were still at home, Meta and Charles. Meta was 17 and an
intelligent girl with long, dark hair. Charles had just turned
15 and although he did not say much, William liked the boy
because he reminded him of Abbie's brother, Willie. There
were seven other children in the Gallon family, all grown and
out on their own.

They were a gregarious group, and soon the wine was
flowing among the adults and there was much laughter and
kidding. William found himself loosening up and telling a few
stories, while the Sheriff shared more than a few of his own.

Meta seemed to laugh the hardest at William talking about his adventures with Edison Electric and the characters he'd met up and down the Eastern seaboard. The Sheriff and Mary exchanged glances at the obvious level of comfort between Meta and William.

After dinner the Sheriff, Percy, and William headed to the front porch to enjoy an after-dinner whiskey and the fine Cuban cigars William had brought as a gift. As they sat in their rocking chairs enjoying the evening light, the Sheriff surprised William with another invitation to come back to the ranch.

"Percy, you need to bring this young man back with you in late October for our fall moose hunt," he told his son.

"Moose? I've never hunted anything like that!" William managed to say, almost choking on his drink. Back in Fall River he and his father occasionally hunted a few ducks and rabbits but nothing bigger than that.

"Don't worry," Percy's father assured him. "We'll help you get everything you will need and show you exactly what to do," he insisted.

"Come with us, William. Dad's right. You have never tasted anything as good as moose meat, I tell you," Percy said, grinning.

William leaned back in his chair, took a long swig of his whiskey, blew a little smoke, and said, "Alright, count me in."

The Sherriff leaned forward, slapped William on the back and said, "You made a good choice, son." Percy just laughed. His father was the most persuasive man he knew.

The men sat together a little while longer in the cool evening before Percy suggested they get some rest. Percy's room was upstairs. William stayed in a guest room that was more like a large closet, but he didn't mind the tight quarters. It had been ages since he'd last had drinks with friends, and to his surprise he had enjoyed it. William went to sleep immediately and awoke the next morning hungry.

As Meta helped her mother prepare a huge breakfast, the Sherriff, Percy, and William sat drinking coffee while Charles slept in. Meta knew her way around a kitchen and effortlessly prepared plates of eggs, bacon, sausage, and a big pan of biscuits with gravy.

"William, do you have a rifle?" the Sherriff asked.

"No sir, I don't" he replied.

"Well, right after breakfast, let's ride into Lindsay and get you outfitted with a rifle to shoot your first moose next month. You take it home with you and that way you can practice some before our big hunt," the Sherriff said.

A couple of hours later William was standing in Long's Gunsmith Shop where he plunked down forty-two dollars to become the proud owner of a .44-40 caliber Winchester

Model 1873. The lever action rifle would come to be known as "The Gun That Won the West" in the lower 48. It was a beauty and William was anxious to fire it just as soon as they got back to the ranch. He was a fairly decent shot, at least at the tin cans Percy set up on the top of a fence rail. The Sherriff gave William some pointers, as the Winchester was unlike any other gun he'd ever handled.

When they returned to the house, Percy and William packed up and said their goodbyes to Mrs. Gallon, Meta, and Charles while the Sheriff brought the carriage around for the hour-long ride back to the train station. They arrived back in Toronto, and William thanked Percy for inviting him, adding that the weekend was one of the best times he'd had in many months.

"Just wait until the hunt," Percy said, and they parted ways.

LINDSAY, ONTARIO
Fall 1892

In late November William and Percy were back at the ranch ready for their moose hunt. The next morning, after a long and dark horseback ride in the wee hours before sunrise, the Sheriff dropped William and Percy at opposite ends of a large swamp near the upper end of Kawartha Lake near Long Point. He instructed them to hunker down in the marshy brush and wait.

"Just sit tight," he said. "There are a lot of moose in this area that love the tender grass in the marshes. I'll check back with you this afternoon, boys." And then he grinned. "That is, unless I hear a shot first. Then I'll be here in a flash. Good luck!"

William felt chilled from the cold morning fog hanging over the swamp that was lit only by a half-moon. The sun, the "poor man's blanket," as the Sheriff called it, slowly creeped over the horizon and he waited anxiously for it to warm him.

After two hours of spotting only a few ducks and geese, William suddenly detected some willows faintly moving on the far side of the swamp about 300 yards away. "That's not just the wind..." he thought just before a blondish-brown patch of fur appeared, followed by a huge set of antlers gently rocking the willows. His heart racing, William sat stock still as a huge moose slowly sauntered out into the morning sun, majestic as it munched tender sprigs of marsh grass dotting the shallow water. He had never seen such a large animal, other than the elephant he'd seen as a kid in a traveling circus back in Fall River. This, however, was a moment he swore he'd never forget, alone with this incredible creature in the Canadian wilderness.

His problem was being out of range for his 44-40. He would just have to sit still and hope the moose would work its way within the 100-yard range of his new Winchester. Steadying the barrel on a tree limb, he practiced his aim like the Sheriff had taught him. William slowed his breath on a long exhale, then gently held it while pretending to slowly squeeze the trigger.

As he intently watched the moose graze, William heard a faint rustle of reeds and a splash of water to his right. He slowly turned his head, hoping to see another moose walking within range. But there was no moose, just two of the cutest black bear cubs he had ever seen. Oblivious to William's presence, they played in the grass covering the water about 40 yards away.

He kept a watchful eye on the cubs as they edged closer. When the cubs were only 30 yards away, the wind shifted and began blowing from William's back straight in the cubs' direction. A minute later, the cubs curiously sniffed the air, peering over in his direction although they did not yet see him. Stealing occasional glances and sniffs as they continued to romp around in the water, they meandered ever closer to him. Finally, just shy of 15 yards away, they suddenly spotted him and began yelping and crying at an alarming volume, nervously scurrying about and creating a ruckus.

Suddenly their mama came crashing out of the willows some 40 yards away, running straight toward her alarmed cubs. William couldn't believe how fast the giant beast moved. She reached her cubs in seconds, then immediately rose on her hind legs, sniffing the air and snapping her jaws. She was on to William's scent, and she meant business.

He was terrified. Hoping she might turn and leave if he

fired over her head, he swung his Winchester in her direction. Noting the sudden movement, her eyes locked onto him, and she instantly dropped to all fours, charging straight at him with fury.

William stood his ground and yelled, his arms shaking as he aimed his weapon. At a mere ten yards, she came to a halt and again stood on her hind legs, snapping and growling at him and saliva dripping from her mouth. It was now or never, William thought. He placed the bead of his rifle right on her chest and squeezed the trigger. The Winchester exploded, and the old sow reeled backwards as smoke from the barrel hung in the morning air.

To William's horror, the furious bear quickly rose seemingly undeterred, once again charging her prey. He quickly worked the lever, chambering another round, and fired again. This time the bear crumpled to the ground in a heap of dark fur, a mere few yards separating them. William chambered a third round and stepped closer to her, but it was not needed as she lay motionless in front of him. Frozen in place, he could not move, aghast at what had just happened. His hands trembling and his breathing heavy, hot tears of relief filled his eyes, and he began shaking uncontrollably before silently sinking to the ground, staring at the massive bear in front of him. He waited there until Sheriff and Percy, who had heard his shots, arrived a half hour later.

"Did you get you a moose, Willie?" Percy yelled as he came into sight through the brush.

William stirred to his feet and yelled back, "Nope! Not a moose, but a really big bear that almost had me for breakfast."

The Sherriff was not far behind. William breathlessly explained what had happened as Percy and his dad inspected the dead bear.

"Wow, she's a big one alright," the Sherriff said, whistling low. "One of the biggest I've ever seen in these parts. She's old and not going to taste so good. But Willie, you've got yourself a nice rug and a hell of a good story to tell your grandkids someday."

William's thoughts briefly drifted to his six-month-old son 700 miles away in Fall River, Massachusetts, and wondered if he would ever have grandchildren to tell.

⊷⊨⊙ ⊙⊨⊶

After skinning, butchering, and packing the bear back to the ranch, the men presented the meat to Mrs. Gallon who did her best to prepare a nice dinner of bear roast. But as predicted, the old sow was tough and greasy. William did his best to smile and compliment her cooking skills, but he was less than convincing as they all reviewed the day's events. Charles kept asking to hear the story again and again as Meta attentively listened.

The next morning William and Percy left on the train for Toronto, declining the Sheriff's invitation to take some bear steaks back with them. The Sheriff promised to get the hide tanned and give it to William on his next visit, which he hoped would be soon. Percy's sister, Meta, was standing in the doorway as the men left, secretly sharing her father's hopes.

William and Percy finally arrived back in Toronto that evening. They were both exhausted, but in an odd way William felt refreshed at the same time. The hunt had been one of the most exciting adventures of his life, yet he had mixed feelings. He was surprised how often thoughts of seeing that mother bear die replayed in his mind. "What happened to her two cubs?" he wondered as he unpacked that evening. He'd worried a thousand times what would become of Leonard now that his mother had died. Would the cubs make it on their own? Would Leonard?

The more he thought about it, the more William became convinced that he and his son were survivors. He had survived the bear attack, he reminded himself. And Leonard had survived his mother's death. Whatever happened next, William swore to make sure they both made it. Tired of feeling sad and overwhelmed with grief, William decided that evening that he had to get on with his life. He was just thirty years old with his whole life ahead of him. It was time.

As the fire died down to embers, William got up from his chair and walked over to the fireplace. He stared at Abbie's painting of Fingal's Cave above the mantel. So far away, yet such a short time ago, he thought. With wet eyes he slowly reached up and gently, almost reverently, removed the painting from its place. He carefully wrapped the painting in a sheet, then a grey felt blanket and gently placed it in the closet. Finding two square ten-penny nails, he drove them into the mortar above the mantel and hung his Winchester 1873 rifle where the painting had been.

Tomorrow would be a new day. He was going to live the rest of his life as best he could without letting the mire and misfortunes of the past weigh him down. That night he went to bed and slept better than he had since Abbie's death seven months prior.

⊷⊨◉ ◉⊨⊶

FALL RIVER, 1894

In Fall River, William's sister cared for Leonard as if he were her own. Lulie loved that little boy and so did her two other children, Lottie and Fred, who had readily adopted him as their own baby brother. Lulie wrote William faithfully as the first years went by, telling him all about Leonard—how cute he was and what a good baby he was, taking note of his first words and his first steps.

William looked for opportunities to visit his young son whenever possible. One such opportunity came in October of 1894 when Lulie married her second husband, William M. Sunderland, (1864-1936). William planned to attend the wedding and couldn't wait to see Leonard who was now two years of age.

Lulie and Leonard met William at the train station, and they had a great time catching up over lunch at the Brayton Avenue Cafe. Leonard squirmed happily in his father's arms and seemed fascinated with the dollar gold piece in William's pinky ring, touching and turning it relentlessly. Lulie told her brother about her fiancé whom William had yet to meet. He was a letter carrier for the post office, Lulie revealed, and they had met one day as he was delivering her mail. After a quick courtship, they decided to marry.

The next day, October 11, 1894, they married in First Congregational Church in Fall River. William sat in the front row with his parents who held Leonard, alongside Lottie and Fred. He did not doubt that Sunderland loved Lulie, but he didn't seem as interested in her children, including Leonard. This observation concerned William, but he appeared to be an otherwise decent man. The family Lulie had cobbled together was an unusual arrangement, but everyone tried to make it work as best they could. Time would tell.

—◦→▭◦ ◦▭←◦—

TORONTO, CANADA 1895

William returned to Toronto and threw himself into his work with abandon. His dedication paid off, and he quickly rose in the ranks to become District Engineer for the Edison Electric Company for the entire Dominion of Canada. William and Percy remained close friends and spent many weekends at the Gallon family ranch in Lindsay. Three years after Abbie's death, William proposed to Percy's little sister, Meta Ann. The two married in a small ceremony at her family's ranch on February 20, 1895. Charles and Percy were William's best men.

William and Meta made their home in Toronto, but after two years William was offered an opportunity that he could hardly pass up. The owners of a newly formed electric railway company in Lorain, Ohio, asked him to head up the development of a new interurban electric rail line running 200 miles along the southern shore of Lake Erie. In 1897 Lorain was a small, up-and-coming industrial city at the mouth of the Black River on the southeastern shore of Lake Erie about 25 miles west of Cleveland. As the superintendent of the Lorain & Cleveland Electric Railway Company, he would be in charge of the construction and operation of an exciting and modern system of electric rail transportation between Cleveland, Lorain, Sandusky, Norwalk, Fremont, Toledo, and Detroit.

With some misgivings, he advised Mr. Edison in a letter that he was leaving the company for this new opportunity in Lorain, on the other side of Lake Erie 300 miles away. To his relief, Mr. Edison was not surprised and wrote him a short congratulatory note accepting his resignation. The letter read in part:

> *We will miss you here at the Company, but I am not surprised that others have sought you out to do for them as you have done for us in expanding the wonders of electricity across the country. I wish you the very best and hope we can stay in close contact in the years ahead…*

It was signed, "Yours truly, Thomas." Although it was difficult for Meta to leave her family behind in Canada, they also gave their blessing.

One summer evening shortly after their move, William broached a sensitive issue with Meta that had been eating on him. Although they had been trying for many months, they had not yet been able to have children, something Meta was desperate to make happen.

"Darling, can I ask you something?" he began, speaking softly to his wife. "I was wondering what you would think about us bringing Leonard into our home and raising him. After all, he is my son, and I feel like I owe him that now that you and I are married and settled here in Lorain. The schools are better here. Leonard's a good boy. And I think the two of you would get along famously."

He glanced up at Meta who was listening but saying nothing. He decided to lighten the moment and added smiling, "Besides, when we have children, they would already have a big brother to look out for them."

Meta smiled at this. She was taken aback, but she could tell this meant a lot to her husband. "William," she said, "I do love you. And if it means that much to you, I am willing to give it a try."

William was surprised at her quick response. He had expected much discussion, but now the issue seemed settled. Grinning from ear to ear, William took Meta in his arms, kissed her, and said, "You will be the best mother ever. Thank you, darling."

William was thrilled with the idea, perhaps more so than Meta. The next day, William wrote to Lulie and told her he planned to send for Leonard so that he could enroll him in school in Lorain that fall. Lulie read William's letter slowly as the thought "Indian giver" came to mind. She was heartbroken. To think, she was now losing the child she had raised for the last five years. By now he seemed as much her child as William's. Still, she understood William's desire to raise his own son and, in many ways, even admired it.

Sunderland thought William's plan was a grand idea when she told him about the letter as they retired for the evening. Her husband reminded Lulie that William was no longer a struggling single father. "Meta can raise Leonard as easily as you can, Lulie. And don't forget that William has a lot more money than we do. He'll be better off with them," he suggested thoughtlessly, signaling the discussion was over. Lulie reluctantly acquiesced, and in a matter of weeks Leonard was on a train in the care of her older son, Fred, headed to Lorain to live with his father and Meta.

Meta did her best to be a good mother, but she was ill-prepared to deal with an energetic young boy. Things rocked along for a few months, but in December Meta announced she was pregnant with her own first child. Her pregnancy was tough, and she increasingly felt that caring for Leonard was more than she could handle. Near the end of the school year, she confessed to William that she just couldn't handle the pregnancy and a six-year-old.

She had tried to adjust, she pleaded, but she simply could not care for Leonard while starting their own family. "He's really not happy here, William. And neither am I, truthfully," she said. "All Leonard has ever known is Lulie, Lottie, and Fred. He loves you, William, but they have become his family now, and he needs to be with them." Meta was resolute, so William reluctantly agreed to send Leonard back to Fall River. Lulie was elated at this turn of events, but her husband did not share her enthusiasm.

On the 20th of June, William was saying goodbye to Leonard at the same train station where he'd welcomed the boy a year ago. Once again, Lulie had sent Fred on the train from Fall River to bring Leonard back home. William, having lost his son for the second time, returned to his house alone with the same emptiness he had experienced six years earlier when he left Leonard in Fall River the first time. However, the next morning he went to the office and tried to forget about his pain.

On August 10, 1898, Meta gave birth to Louise Ellsworth Davis (1898-1974). Fourteen months later they had their second child, Ruth Ellsworth Davis (1899-1978). William was overjoyed when Louise and Ruth were born, but he often privately thought about Leonard and wondered why his son couldn't have been part of the family as well.

Each time William felt familiar guilt creeping up, he reminded himself of what Meta had said. Leonard belonged in Fall River. He took solace in the fact that Lulie had given his son a family, surrounded by grandparents and an older brother and sister. There was no time to let himself dwell on the past. Instead, he tried as best as he could to enjoy his new family and budding career.

Thirteen years later William and Meta had a third surprise child they named William Edward Davis (1912-1982). By the time this son was born, William had long accepted that Leonard would never be part of their family. But so much had transpired by that time.

⊶⊷

FALL RIVER, MASSACHUSETTS

After the failed move to Ohio, Leonard spent the rest of his childhood in Fall River 700 miles away from his father. Lottie and Fred were grown adults at 19 and 20 years of age when Leonard returned in 1898. Both were spending less time at the family home, leaving Leonard as Lulie's only child at home.

The next 10 years were very special for Lulie, who loved Leonard with all her heart. Nevertheless, she always made sure Leonard understood William was still his real father. She explained how much William loved him and even told him stories at night about the little she knew about Abbie, his mother.

"Your dad and I agreed that it would be best for you to come and live here," she'd told him. "And we love you. You can stay here as long as you're happy here, Leonard. As long as you like."

Leonard loved Lulie more than anything and seemed to understand her assurances. Lulie also made sure that Leonard spent a lot of time with his grandparents, Wallace Davis (1829-1905) and Lydia Westgate Borden (1829-1918). He often stayed over at their big, rambling house and was especially fascinated with his PaPa because he was a good carpenter and mechanic, always puttering around in his workshop. Leonard could spend hours watching him work. Likewise, his grandfather loved teaching Leonard how to use his tools and build things, just as he had patiently done with Leonard's father when he was a boy.

Leonard adored his Nana. She loved to cook for him and doted on the boy to the point that Lulie often chided her not to spoil the child. Holidays were very special, especially Thanksgiving and Christmas when everyone would gather at either Lulie's or Nana and PaPa's house.

William did his best as an absentee father, but they were not close. He wrote letters to his son on a regular basis and made sure Lulie had what she needed to financially care for him. Meta tried to be understanding of the situation and did not mind William's periodic visits to Fall River to visit his son, Lulie, and their aging parents. But Meta never accompanied him on the trips, as she had her hands full raising their own children.

William spent a few cherished days with his son a few times a year when he was little, but with his busy work schedule and his other family, his visits were not nearly as often as he wished. Sometimes he had to travel to the East Coast on business and would always try to spend a day or two in Fall River. Whenever William made it to town, it was always a big celebration. They would all gather at his parents for a picnic or dinner. William noticed the growing bond his son had with his grandfather. PaPa interacted so naturally with his grandson and made William wonder if he wasn't making a special effort to fill William's shoes somehow.

One day he watched Leonard rummaging through PaPa's toolbox in his workshop, peppering his grandfather with questions. "What's this?" he asked, holding up a hammer. "What's that?" And then, "Can I build something?"

It brought back memories of how his father had done

the same thing with him when he was Leonard's age. That old toolbox was a treasured memory of his childhood, and William hoped Leonard would carry those same memories with him all his life. Maybe it would even spark an interest in building things, as it had for William who often credited spending time with his father in his workshop for his later interest in engineering.

In late October 1902 William made a trip to New York on business and once again decided to stay over for the weekend in Fall River. On Friday afternoon he rolled into town in time for dinner at his parents' house. Lulie, Lottie, and Fred were there with Leonard, but Lulie's husband had other plans. William was struck by how much his parents were showing their age, as was Lulie. His parents were both 73 by now, and his sister was 42. Even Leonard was starting to fill out at 10 years of age. As they sat around the table after dinner, someone mentioned how fast the time was passing. It was already Halloween, and Thanksgiving was just around the corner.

Leonard piped up, "Somebody needs to tell us a scary story for Halloween!"

Lottie was the first to take the bait. "Well, I know a true story. And there aren't any ghosts, but it's really scary. Are you sure you want to hear it?"

"Yes! Tell it, please tell it!" Leonard begged and the adults chuckled. Nana rolled her eyes. "Oh boy," she thought to herself. "I know what's coming, and I'm tired of hearing it!" But she didn't say anything to spoil the mood as Lulie dimmed the lights at Leonard's urging.

"Now we're ready, Lottie. Tell it!" he said breathlessly.

In a hushed voice, Lottie began her tale. Ten years ago, she explained, there was a man by the name of Andrew Borden. He lived over on Second Avenue, less than a mile from Nana's house. Mr. Borden had amassed a fortune making caskets, and he'd caused a scandal in town when he got remarried to a younger woman named Abby Gray after the death of his wife.

His spinster daughters lived at the house with their father and Abby. Emma was 41 and Lizzie was 32, and they both despised their wicked stepmother. There were even rumors that the stepmother was trying to persuade Mr. Borden to cut the girls out of his will.

William knew this local story well because one day on August 4, 1892, Mr. Borden and Abby were found bludgeoned to death at home. Each had been struck in the head, neck, and chest over a dozen times with a crude weapon like a hatchet or axe. The police investigation showed Emma was out of town visiting a friend, leaving Lizzie and the housekeeper the only ones at home who could have committed the crime. As William recalled, the housekeeper did not seem a likely suspect. But Lizzie had made no secret of her hatred for her stepmother and that she feared being cut off from her inheritance.

Local police eventually pegged Lizzie with motive and opportunity and arrested her. The grand jury indicted her for the murders, and the district attorney prosecuted her.

Leonard hung on every word as Lottie spun the story. "There was a big trial right here in town," she said. "And the jury…"

"Did they find Lizzie guilty?" Leonard interrupted.

"Well, Lizzie hired a fancy lawyer for a lot of money. And the jury ended up letting her off," Lulie interjected. "Everyone believes she did it, of course. And you know what, Leonard? She and her sister still live in that spooky old house on Second Avenue!"

At this, Fred chimed in, "That's right, Leonard. Some people say they've even seen Lizzie roaming around town late at night. Sometimes you can even hear her talking to herself."

"What's she say?" Leonard wanted to know.

"Well, if you listen really closely, she's chanting the same thing over and over," Lottie said. She and Fred then chanted together:

Lizzie Borden took an axe

And gave her mother forty whacks.

When she saw what she had done,

She gave dear old father forty-one.

Lottie and Fred tried not to laugh. "So be careful when you walk home tonight, Leonard," Fred warned. "Stay away from the old Borden house, or else Lizzie Borden might get you."

"Oh, that's not real," Leonard protested before adding, "Is it?"

Everyone laughed.

"Well, you'd better ask your Nana," Lottie replied.

"Nana murdered someone?" Leonard was really getting scared now.

Lulie put her hand on Leonard's arm. "No, she did not. Nana's last name was Borden before she married Papa. She's related to Lizzie Borden, that's all."

"But be sure you ask her nicely because I've heard she sleeps with an axe under her pillow too!" Lottie whispered low.

"Hush, Lottie!" Nana chided as she got up from the table to turn up the lights.

"Oh, son. They're just teasing you," William told Leonard and put his arm around him.

Nana had, of course, followed the trial and she'd heard the

town rumors. She also knew her family had always thought Lizzie to be a little off from the time she was a little girl. She'd also seen Lizzie a time or two over the years, wandering aimlessly around town.

"If I were you," Nana said, reaching over to tickle Leonard in the ribs, "I'd hold your Lulie's hand real tight on the walk home."

"Nana, you're just trying to scare me," Leonard complained before looking over at Lulie. "Can I just stay here tonight? Then maybe we can all walk home together in the daytime tomorrow?"

Everyone roared as Lulie, Lottie, and Nana started to clear the table.

<hr/>

CLEVELAND, OHIO 1905

When William returned home to Lorain, he threw himself back into his electric railway project with great vigor. Much of the 200 miles of line had been built by this time. The electrification was almost complete, but there was still so much to do. William loved working on the cutting edge, and his reputation as a leader in the industry was really taking off.

He was also making an excellent living and amassing considerable wealth from his income, which he invested wisely. He continued writing to his sister and to Leonard, while providing generous support. Nevertheless, Leonard missed his father more than ever when he became a teenager.

After completing the electric railway from Cleveland to Detroit in 1905, William had a new opportunity to join the Cleveland Construction Company. The company was a national leader in building electric power and railway systems throughout the United States, Canada, and the West Indies. In this new job, he would oversee the development of electric power generation and distribution systems at a time of unprecedented growth. He readily accepted.

William and Meta moved their family from Lorain to Cleveland, where they would remain for the rest of their lives. They settled into a good life and soon became prominent in the community. For Christmas in 1908, he surprised Meta and the girls when he pulled in the driveway and honked the horn of a brand-new Ford Model T that he had just purchased as a surprise for the family.

The automobile had debuted a few months earlier in October 1908, and Meta and the girls were the very first of their friends to have one. The Model T was the talk of the town, and William was fortunate to get one of the first ones manufactured because of his friendship with Henry Ford, the founder of the Ford Motor Company. He knew Ford from years ago during his time working on the electric railway line to Detroit. Ford had promised William one of the first new cars off the assembly line, and he'd made good on that promise. William smiled from ear to ear at his family's joy and excitement as they inspected the car, and for a brief moment he felt a real sense of contentment from his success as a father and provider.

The heavy burden of responsibility at work took its toll, however. His days were long, his nights short, and there was a lot of business travel. Despite his best efforts, he was starting to feel his age creeping up on him. Although he was only 47 in 1909, he felt much older. One evening in April that year while closing his office for the day, he felt an odd sensation like tingling in his left arm. He wondered if his arm had gone to sleep after too many hours sitting at his drafting table. As he rose to his feet, he also felt light-headed while gathering his coat and briefcase. He sat down again, took a deep breath, and noticed that his heart was racing, and his jaw also felt tight. What was happening to him? He did not know, but after resting for several minutes the sensation passed. Like he had done a dozen times before, he told himself once more that he needed to find a way to slow down. But he didn't find a way and was soon back into his frenzied way of life.

⊷╾◉ ◉╼⊷

FALL RIVER, MASSACHUSETTS 1910

In February 1910 tragedy struck again. Lulie died unexpectedly after a brief illness. William's sister was only two years older than he was. It seemed impossible that she could have died first. They had lost their father five years earlier, but he had lived a long life at 76 years of age. Lulie was only 49 when she died, which rendered the news that much more shocking. William was devastated, but his first thought was of the children—Leonard, Lottie, and Fred.

William made immediate plans to travel to Fall River for her funeral. When he arrived at the train station, he saw Lottie first and then a handsome young man standing next to her. William hardly recognized the boy he had last seen at his father's funeral in 1905. Had it really been five years since William had been home to Fall River?

Seventeen-year-old Leonard was no longer a gangly adolescent but tall with wide shoulders. As Leonard stepped forward to shake his father's hand, William immediately recognized Abbie's smile on his son's rugged face. William ignored Leonard's outstretched hand and embraced his son, who seemed to stiffen in his father's embrace as if he were not expecting such affection.

After dropping Lottie at the house, the two of them went to lunch. Leonard told his father more details about

Lulie's illness and death. It was obvious to William how much his son was going to miss her, and it hit him once more what a selfless sacrifice his sister had made in raising Leonard from infancy. Lulie was the only mother Leonard would ever know, and he grieved her death tremendously. To comfort Leonard, William talked about how much his sister had meant to them both throughout their lives. Brought together by grief, father and son bonded that afternoon in a way William did not anticipate but was nevertheless grateful for.

That evening William joined his widowed mother for a quiet dinner, consoling her as best he could. But the house that had once held so much laughter was now eerily quiet.

After dinner they reminisced about William's father. "Leonard always goes to his PaPa's workshop and piddles around with the tools," she told William. "Son, promise me something. I want Leonard to have PaPa's toolbox and tools someday, probably after he gets settled into his own home. See that he gets them when he's ready, as I may not be here when that happens."

William was touched. "Mother, I promise you that I will make that happen when the time is right," he assured her.

Six years later when his mother passed away, William gathered all of his father's tools, packed them in the toolbox and had it shipped to Leonard who was by then 24 years of age, married, and gainfully employed.

⊷≔◉≕⊶

The next day at Lulie's funeral service, the whole family gathered, including her mother and her husband, Sunderland. Fred and Lottie and Lottie's fiancé, James McLeod, sat on the front row next to William and Leonard. Next to them was William's other sister, Rhoda, who had arrived in Fall River late the night before.

Many friends of the family filled the wooden pews at the First Congregational Church and listened as the pastor recounted Lulie's quiet but remarkable life. William went forward and spoke briefly of his love for his sister, especially because of what she meant to "their" son, Leonard. Afterward, people made their way to the cemetery for the graveside service. Lulie was laid to rest next to her father and, at her request, next to her first husband, Fred Read. William thought his sister's decision a little odd but said nothing to Sunderland as they stood beside each other at Lulie's grave.

Back at Lulie's house, with just the two of them sitting alone at a picnic table in the backyard, William was surprised Leonard brought up his mother's relationship with Sunderland.

Leonard explained that Lulie had entrusted her mother with the unusual request to be buried next to Fred, and her mother had carried out her wishes.

"The strange thing is that he did not seem to mind that she did that," Leonard noted.

William nodded, his silence bidding Leonard to say more.

"I've never gotten along with him," Leonard confessed, avoiding his father's eyes and instead concentrating on his father's familiar gold pinky ring. "He's not a bad person, don't get me wrong. But he never seemed to care much about any of us kids." Leonard then explained that Sunderland had recently told him in no uncertain terms that it was time for him to move out of the family home and find work.

"I guess I'm on my own hook now," he said, recalling the times Lulie had assured him he could stay at home in Fall River as long as he wanted to. That was over now because his stepfather wanted him out.

Leonard seemed wistful and almost despondent, but no sooner had he spoken those words than he straightened his shoulders and added, "But that's alright by me. I'm ready to get out and make a life for myself."

William did not know many teenagers with that kind of maturity, and it impressed him. Lulie had done a fine job of raising this boy and had somehow made sure that he had everything he needed to become a man before she allowed herself to get sick and die. It was as if she'd finally finished her work and was ready for a rest.

"Son," William offered, "you'll never understand how proud I am of you. I know Lulie was too. And I realize that we don't talk much about the fact that you never knew your mother…" William paused, not certain that he should continue. "But I'll bet Abbie is looking down from heaven right now thinking the same thing about how proud she is of you" he said, his voice breaking and eyes watering.

Leonard stared emotionless at his father. His father had rarely breathed his mother's name, much less talked about her this way.

"Leonard, I want you to know that you are not 'on your own hook.' I am your father, and I will help you any way I can. As soon as I get back to Cleveland, let me check with some friends. Let's see if I can't find you something to help you get started on making that life for yourself. I love you, son."

Hearing his father say he loved him reminded Leonard that he had never felt this close to his father—or any man in his life. Honestly, he didn't quite know how to take it. So he did the first thing to came to his mind. He reached across the table, squeezed his father's hand, and said, "I love you, too" before adding, "…Dad."

DETROIT, MICHIGAN 1910

Within the month, Leonard packed his belongings and boarded a train heading for Detroit, Michigan. Through his father's connections, he'd landed a job with the Detroit United Railway Company as an electrician in its streetcar shop. Wiring street cars was a humble beginning, but it was a job and a start. He was finally on his own and working for a living. Leonard determined to put his head down and work hard to learn all he could as quickly as possible. At the least, he could make his own way from this point forward.

Leonard proved to have an affinity for learning the fundamentals of electricity from the ground up as he wired streetcars in Detroit. He was like a sponge, soaking up everything he could about electricity—how it worked, where it came from, and what it was useful for. He may not have had a college education, but he certainly aspired to do more than wire streetcars for the rest of his life. Thankfully, his bosses liked him and without his knowledge gave regular good reports to his father on his progress.

For now, Leonard enjoyed living in Detroit. It was much bigger than Fall River, and he took advantage of the many things that life in the big city could offer a young man. He also appreciated that Detroit was only a five-hour train ride from his father's home in Cleveland, and he was able to visit on holidays.

One Thanksgiving in 1911, he arrived at his father's house in Cleveland, which was huge by Fall River standards. Martha, the family's domestic servant who lived with them, opened the front door to welcome Leonard. She took his coat and hat as usual and showed him to the living area where his father jumped to his feet and heartily greeted his son as he always did. Despite his father's warm welcome, Leonard felt more like an outsider than a member of the family whenever he visited. And to his disappointment, Meta didn't do much to relieve that feeling. On the surface she was nice enough to Leonard, especially when his father was around. But her actions always seemed a bit contrived. Meta's two daughters were now in their early teens and all-consuming of her attention. Leonard was shocked when his father told him that Meta was pregnant with a third child to be born in the spring. It seemed odd that his father at 49 and Meta at 36 would be having another child, and he took the news to mean that he would be less a part of the family than ever.

Meta had invited some friends and relatives to join them for Thanksgiving dinner later that evening, and it was crowded and warm in the ornate living room as they awaited the meal. Just as everyone was moving to the over-sized dining room, Meta drew Leonard aside.

"Leonard, we don't have enough room at the dining table for everyone. I was wondering if you would be a sweet boy and eat with Martha in the kitchen? I mentioned it to your father, and he said he didn't think you would mind, as you really like Martha."

Leonard, not knowing what else to say, just mumbled, "Sure, no problem." But Meta's casual dismissal stung. Wasn't he good enough to eat with the family? Nevertheless, he ate his plate of turkey and dressing in the kitchen all alone, while Martha busily served everyone else in the next room. It was a long ride back to Detroit at the end of the holiday weekend, and he considered never returning to his father's house.

On March 20, 1912, Meta gave birth to Leonard's half-brother, William Edward Davis. Leonard was even more threatened by the fact that the new baby was named after his father and assumed he would soon take his place as his father's son. Leonard hid his apprehensions and politely congratulated his father and Meta, but where did this latest addition leave him? He did not know.

On his first visit to Cleveland to see his new half-brother in person, Leonard was unusually reserved around his dad. His father could tell something was wrong and took Leonard aside that afternoon to reassure him. He was still just as much his son as the new baby, William explained. However, William's assurances did little to assuage Leonard's fears. As much as his father tried to show him that he loved him, it didn't make up for all the missed years during Leonard's formative years growing up in Fall River. Time that this new son would have.

Leonard understood William was sorry for the time he'd missed and told his father as much. But no matter what words were exchanged, the pain was still there, where it remained for the rest of Leonard's life.

In late April 1912, it was William's turn to visit Leonard up north. He came to Detroit on business and took his son to a fancy restaurant for dinner. Leonard looked forward to seeing his father. It would finally be just the two of them without the rest of the family. After they ordered dinner, William seemed anxious to talk to his son about something important.

"I've been hearing good things about how you are doing at the railcar shop," his father began. "They say you are a hard worker and that you catch on quick." It was true. Leonard was a natural at electrical wiring, something he'd picked up from hours spent watching his grandfather in his shop.

"How would you like to go to Texas and work on a new electric power plant we are building down there?" William asked, cutting into his steak. "Many people think of Fort Worth as nothing but a cow town, but it's growing by leaps and bounds. You'd be working for the Fort Worth Light and Power Company. I believe there is a lot of opportunity there for a young man with your abilities, son."

Leonard didn't hesitate. "Texas? Shoot, Dad. When do I leave?"

William laughed. "Well, a lot of people are going there to seek their fortune, given all that's happening with oil and industry in Texas. So you want to get in on the ground floor of this thing?"

"Count me in. I won't let you down," Leonard said, eager to prove himself.

"Good enough, son," his father said. "They say they need

you right away. So as soon as you can clear out with the Detroit Railway, you get on down to Texas." His father then explained that Leonard would need to be in place by the first of June at the latest. "With that new plant about to come online, they are needing lots of help," he added.

Leonard, grinning from ear to ear, raised his glass of wine and said, "Goodbye Detroit, hello Texas!"

William smiled, remembering his own youthful enthusiasm when he was first starting out with Edison. If Lady Luck were on his son's side, this move to Texas could prove to be a very good thing for him.

◦◦▸▦◉ ◉▦◂◦◦

FORT WORTH, TEXAS
Spring 1912

On May 20, 1912, Leonard boarded a train in Detroit carrying everything he owned in one suitcase. It was a long two-day trip, but Leonard enjoyed seeing the heartland of America as the train rolled its way south. As they crossed the Red River from Oklahoma into Texas, the topography changed and Leonard saw nothing but barren prairie sprinkled with small brush and a few trees. The sun streamed in through the window and the small car grew hotter and hotter the

172

further south they traveled, and it was only May. Texas was far different than the cooler climate and lush, green landscape Leonard was accustomed to in Massachusetts and Michigan. But he decided the South had a rugged beauty all its own as he admired its vastness.

Maybe this is a good move, he reminded himself and set aside any lingering doubts. As the train rambled into the Texas and Pacific Railway Station in Fort Worth, he grew nervous with anticipation. The steam of the engine hissed as Leonard stepped off the train, taking his first step onto Texas soil and into what he hoped would be a new life.

At that time, Fort Worth was much smaller than Detroit and was a relatively new city. It had been settled a mere 62 years earlier in 1850 with the establishment of a fort at the confluence of the Clear and West Forks of the Trinity River. Over a hundred brave homesteaders had come West to stake their claims and lived as close as possible to the fort, as they depended on it for protection from the Indians whose land they were now trying to farm.

By 1873 the population of Forth Worth had grown to only 500 and was mainly a resting place for cowboys driving great herds of Longhorn cattle on the Chisholm Trail from Texas up to the railheads in Kansas City. Settling their lowing herds outside the city limits to enjoy the clear water of the Trinity

River, the younger cowboys headed into town, galloping their horses and firing pistols into the air on the way to spending their brief break drinking and partying in the saloons. An infamous red-light district sprang up and became known as "Hell's Half-Acre."

A few years later in 1876 things started to settle down when the Texas and Pacific Railroad extended its railroad line into Fort Worth. This move made the city a proper destination for businessmen and families. By 1900 Fort Worth's population had reached 26,000, but the growth really took off when someone asked why Fort Worth was shipping its cattle to be slaughtered in Kansas, instead of butchering them right there in Fort Worth to secure its own piece of the growing meat-packing business in America.

Packing houses sprung up overnight, and by 1902 Swift & Company and Armour & Company employed thousands of workers. By 1910 the population tripled to over 76,000 and the town earned its official nickname: "Cowtown." Fort Worth became known the world over as "Where the West Begins."

The powerful smell of cattle was the first thing Leonard noticed as a carriage took him to a local hotel on the north side of the Trinity River. The rich odor of thousands of cows was pungent. That, along with manure, crowded stockyards, and packing plants created a unique ambiance that anyone, especially a newcomer, could not help but notice. He ate some dinner in the hotel and fell asleep early.

The next morning Leonard found a small apartment to rent just north of town near his work. Ten days later on June 1, 1912, he clocked in as a laborer helping install five boxcars of electric power generating equipment that had just arrived in town in town for the new power plant. Over the coming months, Leonard would get his hands dirty learning all about electric power generation, from the grimy basement to the top of the smokestack.

⋅⊷══◉ ◉══⊶⋅

The site for the new North Main Electric Power Plant that his father's company, the Cleveland Construction Company, was building for Forth Worth Light & Power was the talk of the town. Two years prior to Leonard's arrival in Fort Worth, William had made his own trip to Texas in 1910 to present his group's plans to the city commissioners.

In the sweltering heat that summer, William had trudged up the steps of the Tarrant County courthouse on August 23, 1910. He paused on the third step to admire the newly constructed Renaissance Revival style of the structure. It towered

194 feet above him and was constructed of pink granite all the way up to its pinnacle clock tower. Many people often compared the Fort Worth courthouse to the equally impressive state capitol building in Austin. Surely a town that could build such a courthouse was forward-thinking enough to recognize the future need for electric power, he reasoned. It was William's first trip to Fort Worth, and he was surprised that such a small town held such great promise.

When William entered the courtroom, he took a seat at the front table on the right. He rose to his feet as the six commissioners entered and took their seats behind the bench. The clerk began the proceedings by reciting the minutes of the last meeting, which were quickly approved.

She then announced, "The commission recognizes Mr. William E. Davis, vice-president of the Cleveland Construction Company, regarding a proposed new city power plant."

"Good morning gentlemen," William began, rising to his feet before proceeding to deliver the speech he'd rehearsed the whole way down to Texas.

"I am here today as the representative of Mr. J. R. Nutt of the Citizens Saving and Trust Company of Cleveland, Ohio. As you know, Mr. Nutt recently purchased the electric franchises of the Fort Worth Light and Power Company and the Consumer Light and Lighting Company of your good community. His syndicate has great plans to turn these two fledgling electric companies into the largest electric power generation and distribution system in the entire Southwest. He is prepared to invest the sum of $1,000,000 to construct a new state-of-the art power generation plant just across the Trinity River from this very beautiful courthouse. In fact, he has already purchased the tract of land for the plant near the junctions of the East and West Forks of the Trinity River."

William tried to sense the reaction of the commissioners, then continued with more specifics.

"The plant will be constructed entirely of concrete and brick with the main building being 65 feet in height and the smokestack towering 265 feet. Three 4,000-kilowatt steam turbine-driven generators, each weighing 150 tons, will be installed in the plant. And each one will generate more power than the three existing antiquated plants of the two companies Mr. Nutt has just purchased."

Several men nodded in agreement with this improvement over the current system.

"The steam for the turbine-driven generators will be supplied by three massive boilers that will be arranged so that either coal, gas, or oil can be used as fuel. We will build a dam on the Trinity River to provide the water for the boilers. In addition to the power generation plant, we will be heavily investing in the installation of new electric distribution lines within Fort Worth and transmission lines to carry electric power a distance of 150 miles south to neighboring towns and farms.

"Once it's completed, gentlemen, this new power plant will have a capacity of over 10,000 horsepower and will make Fort Worth the greatest electric power generation center in the entire Southwest. Imagine putting affordable electric lights within the reach of everyone, from homeowners to farmers. I am here to respectfully ask you to approve this project by granting us permission to construct the plant, build the dam, and install the electric distribution and transmission lines both underground and overhead within existing city-owned rights-of-way.

The commissioners were listening intently to William's presentation. He wanted to leave them with a commonsense rationale for why they should approve the project.

"Gentlemen, I have been doing this a long time, starting with Thomas Edison's company, Edison Electric, in New York. We've done business throughout the Eastern seaboard, the Great Lakes, and the Dominion of Canada. I can assure you that this is a sound project. It is well financed and will be successful for both our company and your town. I'd be happy to answer any questions you might have," William concluded.

There were many questions and a lot of enthusiasm for the project. After a few minutes of discussion back and forth, the commissioners unanimously approved the proposal, shook hands all around, and all adjourned to the Texas Hotel to celebrate the agreement.

Over the next two years, William would make many trips from Cleveland to Fort Worth to oversee the planning and construction of the new power plant. A capable construction superintendent oversaw the project day to day, but as vice-president William shouldered the overall responsibility. He enjoyed interacting with the town's leadership, as well as the executives of Mr. Nutt's newly acquired Fort Worth Light and Power Company which would be taking over operation of the plant. In his usual affable style, William formed fast friendships with all the players, and his likability proved instrumental to the success of the project.

⊷⊨⊜ ⊜⊨⊶

FORT WORTH, TEXAS
Summer 1912

By the summer of 1912, it was all coming together just in time for Leonard to begin working at the plant. Construction had taken longer than William had initially thought, and the cost was $500,000 more than the exorbitant sum of a million dollars originally estimated, but it was worth it. The plant's building and accompanying dam were now complete, and the massive boilers and turbine electric generators would soon be installed.

While his father met with executives in suits and ties, Leonard was hands-on in the installation phase of all the newly arrived equipment and wiring. No one knew he was the boss's son, and he didn't necessarily want them to know it either.

On November 1, 1912, Leonard watched from the back of the crowded Main Generator Hall as the city and county commissioners, the executives of Fort Worth Light and Power Company, and J.R. Nutt and his father all stood on the podium for the dedication and grand opening of the new power plant. Politicians and executives alike spoke with great praise and excitement for what this enormous endeavor would do for Fort Worth and Texas.

Leonard smiled to himself when Mayor W.D. Davis concluded his remarks by thanking his father. "I'd like to now recognize the one man who has made this entire project succeed," Mayor Davis began. "His name is Davis, just like mine, but no relation I assure you." The crowd laughed and applauded.

"William, come on up here. Folks, I am honored to

introduce the Vice-President of the Cleveland Construction Company, Mr. William E. Davis."

William made his way forward on the platform and stood beside the mayor.

The mayor continued, "He presented this project to us over two years ago. We were impressed with him then, and we are even more impressed with him today. He has been good to his word and has accomplished every task. Through his rugged simplicity and the genial warmth of his personality he has become a true friend to all of us and our town. I'd like to ask him to say a few words, and then we will flip the switch and turn the power on for our great city."

As his father stood at the podium, Leonard felt the pride swelling in his heart.

"Thank you, Mayor Davis," his dad began. "But we could not have done it without you and your fellow commissioners. Your foresight and vision have been impeccable. You have been outstanding to work with. And I congratulate you and your town on this great accomplishment."

The audience applauded.

"You know," William continued, "when I first came to Texas from up North, I didn't know quite what to expect. What was I going to find in this 'cow town' that everyone says marks the place where the West begins? But I must say that

I have grown to love this town and its citizens. As you know, Texas is very unique. In fact, on the way down here on the train I was thinking about that fact, and I jotted down a short poem I titled 'Texas.' I'd like to share it with you, if that's okay. I fancy myself a bit of a poet, although not a very good one. So please bear with me."

William unfolded a piece of paper from his coat pocket and began:

TEXAS

Hats off to you, Texas, your welcoming smile
Is as broad as your prairies are fair.
Your strong hearty handshake is surely worthwhile,
Your "Howdy" a cure for dull care.

The prince and pauper are used just alike,
And used as but Southerners can.
No pedigree asked for,
You're expected to be just a man.

Of course, you find freaks, who complain of the heat,
But they would kick about heaven as well.
The true Texan answers, "It's sure hard to beat,
But, stranger, it's hotter in Hell."

Inspired by that spirit, she's getting her stride,

Just in front of Prosperity's band.

It's never "I can't, but, doggone your hide,

It is "I jest natch'lly can."

So here's to fair Texas, in strength may she grow,

Her Lone Star ablaze in the sky,

While the soft balmy winds of jasmine and rose

Still haunt us, and whisper, "Goodbye."

The crowded roared and applauded their approval when William finished reading the poem.

"So before we flip this switch and see if this big machine will run," he continued, "let me just say in conclusion that as far as I am concerned, my goodbye to this fair city will only be temporary. I hope to see all my new Texan friends again very soon."

Then William turned to the mayor and said, "Mr. Mayor, if you will do the honors, let's turn ol' North Main on and light this city up!"

The mayor stepped forward and threw a giant copper breaker switch to the "on" position, releasing a hiss of steam as the turbines started to tune. The generator started turning faster and faster until the 400 lightbulbs strung overhead flickered to life as the crowd cheered and slapped each other on the back.

Leonard stood speechless. This new plant was really something, he thought to himself as the lights sparkled above him and the crowd whooped and hollered in amazement.

⋅–≡◯⧟–⋅

The next day, Leonard met his father at the Fort Worth Club, a prestigious private club on the top floor of the Fort Worth National Bank with white tablecloths and fine China place settings. Leonard was glad he had worn his best shoes and his only coat and tie. He would later look back on this first lunch there with his father as a treasured memory, but by then he'd become a member of this same club in his own right.

During lunch his father told him of some family news. He'd heard through the grapevine that Sunderland had married a younger woman named Mary Brooks.

"That didn't take long, did it?" Leonard said rather sarcastically.

William nodded. "No, it didn't," he said, noting his son's reticence to talk about his stepfather any further.

They spent the rest of the lunch talking about work. Leonard told his father how much he liked Fort Worth and

184

his job. It had been hard getting the plant ready for the grand opening, but now that the plant was up and running, he wasn't sure what he'd be doing next with the company. Nevertheless, he was excited to find out, even though he had a mountain to climb working his way up from blue-collar jobs if he was ever going to prove himself a success.

"Well, I don't know what you will be doing either, son. But whatever they offer you, just work as hard as you can. Be successful at it, and then other good things will be sure to follow. That's what PaPa always told me, and that's what I've always done. It's worked for me, and I am sure it will for you as well."

They finished lunch and Leonard tucked away his father's advice. A few weeks later he remembered it as he found himself in the pole yard shaving the bark off logs to turn them into light poles for the company's electric distribution system. What a way to start my new job, he thought. As he looked up at the daunting stack of unshaven logs, he knew with certainty that this was not what he wanted to be doing the rest of his life. It was early December, but the weather was unseasonably warm, and he was already wringing wet with perspiration.

As he remembered his father's words, he took a deep breath, pulled off his shirt and went back to shaving bark with a vengeance, telling himself with a smile, "Maybe this will be a great way to work on my summer tan early. And maybe it will even help me meet a pretty girl at Lake Worth this summer!"

His wish came true long before summer and it wasn't at Lake Worth. In February of 1913, a friend from work named Jim George invited him to a Sunday afternoon social at First Christian Church in Fort Worth. Leonard had nothing else to do, so he went, and was he ever glad he did. As he glanced around the room, he caught the eye of the most beautiful young girl he'd ever seen. She was sitting with two other people, and he thought he saw her glancing back at him as well.

"Who's that girl over there?" William whispered to Jim, nodding toward her.

"Oh, that's Esther Martin. She's new to town. I think she's here visiting her older sister, Ida, who's married to Elbert Kelly. They call him Bert, you know." He pointed to a couple sitting next to Esther. "Bert works for the railroad, so they've been here a couple of years. I think they came from Illinois."

"Have you met Esther?" Leonard inquired. "Better yet, could you introduce me to her?"

Jim punched his friend in the arm. "Oh, I get it. Sure, come on," he said, and the two young men wandered over toward the trio sitting in the corner.

"I want you to meet my friend from work," Jim said. "This here is Leonard Davis." Leonard reached over to shake Esther,

Ida, and Bert's hands, and soon Leonard was fetching Esther a cup of punch as the two of them started chatting alone.

Esther told him she was in town visiting two of her married sisters who had moved to Fort Worth with their husbands a few years prior. Esther had grown up in tough circumstances as one of seven children on a farm near Westchester, Illinois, where her father raised corn. When Esther was just four years old, her father, Horace Martin (1846-1897), died unexpectedly leaving her mother with seven children to support and raise by herself.

Her mother, Eliza Jane Smithson (1853-1929), never re-married and had a hard time making it financially as a farmer's widow. The older children pitched in and helped, but it was still hard going for all of them. Esther found herself very easily and naturally confiding in Leonard how her mother had struggled to make ends meet ever since her father's death.

"After Ida and Bert got married," Esther explained, "Bert heard of the opportunities in Fort Worth, and they moved here in 1909." Leonard learned that another one of Esther's sisters named Elsie (who was 26) and her husband Jesse Gibbs (two years older) had also decided to follow them to Texas.

"And now Jesse has a very good job with a local cigar man-ufacturing company," she added. Leonard was listening, but he was primarily thinking about how much he was enjoying just hearing this young lady talk. She had the sweetest voice and was so easy on his eyes.

Esther had graduated from high school last year and was now 19. She and her twenty-three-year-old brother, Herman, were on a visit to Texas and trying to decide whether to stay in Fort Worth with family or go back to Illinois. Leonard hoped with all his might that her decision would be the former and spoke glowingly of life in Fort Worth.

Esther nodded. "There's just not much opportunity in Winchester, and I'm really ready for something with a little more promise for the future," she told Leonard as she sipped her punch.

"But enough about me, what about you?" she asked.

Suddenly he was telling her his life story, too. He talked about Aunt Lulie raising him in Fall River after his mother died in Toronto when he was born. She listened intently when he described growing up with his adopted siblings, Lottie and Fred, and even teared up when he told her about Lulie's death two years prior.

When he mentioned Sunderland kicking him out of the house, Esther looking concerned asked, "What about your real father, Leonard?"

"My father took me under his wing and helped me get started with the Detroit Electric Railway Company in Detroit,"

Leonard replied. "Now I'm working at the Fort Worth Light and Power Company because of my dad's connections," he told her, leaving out the ignominious part about shaving bark off electric poles.

They talked for over two hours in the corner of the church before Esther finally had to leave. "I sure hope you decide to stay in Fort Worth," Leonard ventured. "There really is a lot of opportunity here." He hesitated. "And, you know, I'm here too. And if you didn't mind, I would sure like to kind of see you again."

Leonard should have been nervous being this bold, but he felt strangely calm. Esther blushed a bit, then smiled. "Leonard, are you trying to say you might be part of that opportunity here?"

He laughed and added, "Who knows? Maybe." He asked and she gave him her sister's phone number. Leonard promised to call her, and not too long after, he did.

Leonard and Esther saw a lot of each other for the next six weeks until Esther's visit was cut short. She told him that she had to go back to Illinois because her mother was having health problems and needed help around the house. Esther was torn between wanting to stay in Texas with Leonard and needing to help her mother. Although Leonard could not hide his disappointment, he understood her dilemma.

They said their goodbyes at the train station in April and promised to write as they held each other tight. With a long, lingering kiss they parted ways, not fully knowing, but hoping, that this kiss would not be their last. The steam engine hissed and as the train wheels slowly started to move, Leonard felt the same pang of emptiness in the pit of his stomach that he had felt when he lost his Aunt Lulie. Slowly the train began to move while Esther's sweet face was pressed against the window as they waved goodbye.

FORT WORTH, TEXAS 1912

By the end of 1913, Leonard was no longer coming home with splinters from shaving bark off trees for electric poles. He had secured a new job as a lineman for Fort Worth Light and Power Company. He was now helping install the company's ever-expanding electric distribution lines onto some of those very poles he had shaved the bark off of. It was hard work, digging deep holes for the electric poles, setting them with a crane truck, then stringing electric wires from pole to pole. He acquired the requisite skills, strapping on climbing spikes, throwing a rope around his waist, and working his way to the top of the 30-foot poles to pull the wiring into position.

The climbing work was a bit dangerous, but he enjoyed the challenge and quickly became "monkey-quick" as the other linemen called it. Leonard continued to write Esther and looked forward to checking his mailbox each day for a letter in return.

By December, her mother's health was improving, and she was starting to talk about returning to Fort Worth. Jesse, her brother-in-law, knew about an opening at the Cigar company for a secretarial position. Leonard was keen on the idea and encouraged her to do it. She came to Texas for an interview in January 1914, and her new boss offered her the job on the spot. Esther accepted without hesitation, and Leonard took her to dinner that night at the Brown Derby Restaurant to celebrate.

The year flew by after Esther moved to Texas and started working. She and Leonard saw each other every weekend. By the end of November Leonard mailed a handwritten letter to Esther's mother in Illinois.

1216 Fifth Avenue
Fort Worth, Texas
November 30, 1914

Dear Mother,

You will be greatly surprised to hear me, but nevertheless I consider it my duty to write my future mother-in-law once in a while.

So please take this letter good-naturedly. Yes, I am going to call you mother from now on, as I intend to marry your daughter (Esther) in a very short while, that is, if I may have your consent. So please let me know if you will give me your daughter's hand.

I just finished talking to Esther over the phone and she told me to tell you she loves you as much as ever.

She is a very nice girl, and I could not find a nicer and sweeter girl than Esther, and mother dear, I love her with all my heart and will do my utmost to make her an ideal husband.

You may wish to know about your future son. So here goes. I am one year older than Esther (22, 23 in May) and since my Aunt died in Fall River, Massachusetts I have been on my own hook. My father is still living in Cleveland, Ohio, but as I have a stepmother, I cannot get along at home. But dear Dad is with me and pushing me along in my work.

I am now employed in the office of the Fort Worth Light & Power Company at $85 per month with a prospective raise to $100 the first of the year.

I have been working five years now. I first worked in Detroit, Michigan as an electrician in the Detroit United Railway streetcar shop. I was employed there two years and then father sent me down here, and since my career in Fort Worth I have worked at every branch in the electrical work, and now I have qualified myself to work in the Commercial Department and I have a better object in view in the near future, and with a nice girl as Esther as my wife, I cannot help but gain success.

So please let me know, dear mother, if you give your consent. Hoping to hear from you soon.

With love, I remain,
Your son,

Leonard E. Davis

With a letter like that, he wondered, how could she say no? Fortunately, his future mother-in-law gave her blessing. On

February 22, 1915, Esther and Leonard married in a simple
ceremony at Ida and Bert's house at 401 Lipscomb Street in
Fort Worth. Esther's other sister, Elsie, served as her maid-of-
honor while Elsie's husband, Jesse, was Leonard's best-man.
His father sent his regrets that he would be tied up with business in Cleveland, but he sent his best wishes and enough
money to pay for a honeymoon they could not have otherwise
afforded. While Leonard was disappointed to not have any
family present at the wedding, he felt the love of all of Esther's
family with whom he would remain close for the rest of his life.

After their honeymoon on the Gulf Coast in Galveston,
the newly married couple moved into a garage apartment that
Ida and Bert rented to them at a reasonable rate. Esther continued to work for the Cigar company, and Leonard continued
with Fort Worth Light and Power. Leonard soon earned another promotion, this time in the commercial department as
an electrical engineer. While he enjoyed the engineering side
of it, he thought the best opportunity in the company was in
expanding its customer base by persuading more people to use
more electricity to improve the quality of their lives.

Soon, he found his niche working in the sales end of the
commercial department. He made a real hit with his boss when
he suggested they have a campaign to sell housewives on the
marvels of electric waffle irons. His idea led to a tremendously

successful sales promotion. As his father had predicted, Leonard quickly moved up the ladder. His easy-going manner and earnest nature, coupled with the quick wit of his father, helped the company expand its business to new customers, both residential and commercial.

William was very proud to see his son following in his footsteps. He'd not needed to support his son financially since he married, and he admired his independence and determination to make it on his own.

⊷⇒ ◐⇐⊶

CLEVELAND, OHIO 1913-1920

William's work evolved to the point where at 53 years of age, he was no longer the hard-driving executive he had been only a few years earlier. After sixteen years with Edison Electric Company, eight years with the Lorain & Cleveland Electric Railway Company, and ten years with the Cleveland Construction Company, he was more than ready to slow down. He had built the reputation of having constructed more miles of electric railway than any other engineer in the country and was highly regarded as a leader in the construction of electric power generation plants.

After the successful plant launch in Fort Worth, William

left the Cleveland Construction Company to accept a prominent government appointment as the Commissioner of Light,
Power and Heat for the City of Cleveland, a position he
held from 1913-1920. In the little spare time that he had, he
stretched himself thin between being home with Meta and
their children and his involvement in several social clubs and
organizations. He was a member of several electric and engineering societies because of his influence in the industry. Even
the mayor had asked him to serve on his cabinet. Everyone
seemed to want his opinion or advice. But his main interest
outside of work was being a high-ranking 32nd degree Mason
and serving with other members of this exclusive fraternal
organization.

When his daughter-in-law, Esther, gave birth to his first
grandson on March 3, 1918, they named him William "Bill"
Ellsworth Davis after Leonard's father. William was very
touched that their baby would carry his name. Anxious to meet
his new namesake, William assured the couple that he would
try to get down to Texas as soon as he could. A second child,
Robert "Bob" Leonard Davis, was born two years later in 1920.

Lottie was the godmother of both of Leonard's children,
and they always referred to her as Aunt Lottie. Before Leonard
left Fall River to begin his career, Lottie had married James
Mcleod on March 17, 1910 in the same church where the

family held Lulie's funeral just weeks prior. Leonard was flattered that James, a 22-year-old Scottish immigrant, had asked him to serve as his best man. James was an excellent mechanic and later owned his own garage. In the years after they got married, he and Lottie had four daughters – Louise, Eleanor, Jean, and Eunice. James worked long hours to support his family until his tragic death in 1927 at just 39 years of years of age. Lottie was heartbroken and never remarried, choosing to raise their four children alone.

Perhaps brought together by the shared pain of loss, Lottie and Leonard remained very close throughout the rest of their lives, writing each other on a regular basis and seeing each other whenever possible.

On William's visits to see his grandchildren, he and his son often enjoyed sharing a cigar on Leonard's screened-in porch after dinner and an occasional whiskey. Their relationship had been deepening over the years, and they now laughed with a joy that only a father and son can share, knowing that a third generation of Davis men had begun. William often thought of Abbie when he was with Leonard and knew how proud she'd be that her legacy was being carried forward in Leonard and his two beautiful children, one of which carried his name.

While her life had ended long ago, new lives had begun in her place.

⊷╾◉ ◉╼⊷

CLEVELAND, OHIO 1920-1930

In 1920 at the age of 58 William slowed down even more and semi-retired to private consulting on electrical projects that afforded him more freedom in his schedule. When he finally fully retired in 1929 at the age of 67 years, several of his colleagues and friends worked with Meta to arrange a surprise retirement celebration. After one of his closest friends spoke about his extensive and strenuous working career in the development of electric power, it was obvious to everyone that William had singularly accomplished more work than several men could have achieved over the past half-century.

Less than two percent of America was using electricity when William began his career. But by 1920, American industry had experienced extraordinary expansion. There were more and more power plants across the nation as the use of electricity worked its way into rural areas outside of the big cities. From gas engines to automatic substations and the discovery of superconductivity, electricity was now a practical necessity powering the entire nation. William felt a real sense of satisfaction in all he had done in his career, notwithstanding the hardships he had endured personally. His hard work had changed his own fortune and in many ways the fortunes of many in the country he loved. Millions of Americans and American businesses had benefitted from his contributions and innovations as a pioneer in electric power generation and distribution, and millions more would benefit for generations to come.

At the end of the celebration, William humbly thanked everyone for the well-wishes on his retirement and even joked that it was no wonder he was so tired after seeing the whole evolution of electrical development and at all times being one of the members of it!

Now that William had more time on his hands, his thoughts often turned to his past. He could recall certain memories with such clarity that they seemed as if they'd happened just the other day. Wasn't it just yesterday when he was visiting his three-year-old son, Leonard, at his sister's house in Fall River? They were playing in her front yard with a red ball, and Leonard was as carefree as a boy could be.

But then again, it seemed a lifetime ago when he was the young man walking his future bride, Abbie, to Grandpa Jesse's house, carrying her torn sack of apples in the crook of his arm and talking together as if they'd always known each other. Their honeymoon to Scotland, Fingal's Cave, her painting, Abbie's death, Leonard's birth, taking his son to Lulie's – the thoughts were somehow fresh but far away.

There were other days when his mind drifted to his graduation from high school and walking the hallways of Brown University for the first time. Bookbag in hand, he'd sat in his first college classroom wondering why he was there and what in the world he would do with his life. Now he felt it was growing toward the end.

Strung together, the days seemed to live behind a piece of clouded glass, as if they had happened to someone else. Life was so different then. America was so different then. How could one man's lifetime span it all? But somehow it did just that, and he was part of it all. The problem was that it had all gone by too fast, too quickly.

Those who knew William always saw his jovial smile, but what William kept to himself was the shadow of heartbreak and remorse. The sting of shock and grief he'd experienced as a young husband and new father stayed with him his entire life. He could never work hard enough or long enough to ease the heartache.

Driven by his attempt to erase those memories throughout his long career, he left behind a legacy of total dedication in the electrical industry. However, he never sought personal accolades or attention for himself. It wasn't his way. As he neared the end of his life, he hoped there would be no bitter tears at his eventual passing, wanting only to comfort those who would miss him.

One evening in 1926, William returned once again to his gift of verse to express his reflections on death and dying. He penned a poem he entitled "Requiem," something he wanted read at this funeral.

REQUIEM

When I "pass out" I want no tears,
No grief, no mourning of my kin.
'Tis just Life's cycle made complete,
Perhaps a new one will begin.

A breath of music, soft and low,
A few kind words, an earnest prayer.
No flowers, no pomp, no thought of pain,
I had no fear, for Death was there.

And Death is kind, he asks no wage;
So strong, yet gentle as a dove.
Perhaps he opens wide a door

That we may meet with those we love.

E'en though the future's kindly hid,
A Master Hand to harbor fair
My storm-tossed soul would seem to guide.
I hope we all find refuge there.

And it was. Four years later on October 9, 1930, Leonard was sitting in his office when the call came. "Leonard, this is Meta," a soft voice began on the other end of the line.

He braced himself. She had never called him before.

She continued, "I have some very bad news. Your father passed away this morning at home from a heart attack."

Leonard was silent. They exchanged a few superficial comments about what had transpired, then he hung up the black receiver. Leonard stared into space before the tears started and he sobbed uncontrollably. He was glad the office door was closed. After a few minutes, he gathered himself, dried his eyes, and summoned his secretary. He informed her that his father was dead and asked her to start making train reservations for him to get to Cleveland as fast as possible.

Leonard had a lot of time to think on the train ride. He was now only 38 years old, but he had lost so much. Abbie, the mother he never knew. Lulie, his adopted mother. And now his father, who had helped him when he needed it most. He felt very lost and alone, but he took solace as he pictured Esther and his two young sons back home. When he finally arrived in Cleveland, Louise was waiting at the train station. They quietly shared about their mutual loss on the way to their house at 10503 Lake Avenue in Lakewood, a suburb of Cleveland where many family members and friends had gathered.

William was sorely missed by friends and colleagues alike who poured out their condolences in other gatherings and newspaper articles published in the cities and communities across America and Canada where he'd lived and worked.

Despite William's urging about not mourning him, there were indeed tears at his passing from those who knew and loved him as a husband, devoted father, friend, and colleague. In a lengthy tribute to one of its most best-known citizens the *Cleveland Bystander* tried to capture the community's loss.

> The written word is impotent to portray those innermost characteristics of a man which constitute his spiritual makeup, and the inadequacy of this medium of expression becomes especially

pronounced when directed toward a man of outstanding achievement and unique personality.

Such a man was William Ellsworth Davis,
whose sudden and untimely death at the age of
sixty-seven, from a heart attack on the morning
of October 9, 1930, shocked the entire community. His was a career of accomplishment,
and the impress of his engineering genius will
remain as an abiding influence upon the future
development of that vast industry to which he
so effectively gave his life and effort.

Thus, by cumulative achievement his fame and
reputation in the electric power industry had
become international, but by his countless host
of friends and acquaintances he will be remembered rather for the rugged simplicity and genial
warmth of his personality. He possessed an unusual capacity for friendship, and his sparkling
wit, his jovial and lightning repartee, and his
never-failing optimism made a cherished and
welcome companion wherever he might drop
in. Few men have had his gift of storytelling,

and the facility with which he matched each occasion with an appropriate 'yarn' marked him as a master of the art. He was, indeed, a lovable character, and especially in these days of needless fears and false alarms the world can ill-afford to lose his cheery smile and militant faith.

Leonard listened intently as his father's remarkable life was honored at his funeral. He was particularly struck by the poem his father wrote and wanted read at his funeral.

"No tears, no grief, no mourning of my kin..." He heard his father recite the words from beyond the grave, but it was so hard to comply with his wishes as Leonard's eyes blurred and tears rolled down his cheeks.

Many people attended the funeral and the reception following. But Leonard knew hardly anyone, other than his stepsiblings and stepmother. Meta seemed to be the center of everyone's attention. It was a further shame that most people outside of his family did not even know that William had been married before Meta, given that this information was not included in the obituaries in several newspapers after William's death. This fact was also painfully obvious to Leonard, as he'd had to introduce himself many times at the visitation the night before. Again, he was part of the family, but at the same time he clearly wasn't, and the push-pull of emotions brought back a lot of bad feelings.

At the reception, he shook hands with a colleague of William's from his time at the Edison Company. This man had traveled from New York to Cleveland to pay tribute to his father.

"William was a great man," he told Leonard. "How did you know him and the family?"

Leonard was taken aback. "Well, I'm his son, Leonard," he answered.

The man's neck turned red, and his eyes widened. "Well, I didn't know William and Meta had an older boy. My apologies, son," the man stammered.

"Not Meta…" Leonard began before stopping himself. "Never mind. It's alright. Thank you for coming," Leonard assured the man before excusing himself to get a drink of water.

Leonard loosened his tie, feeling suddenly very uncomfortable in his black suit. Who was he trying to fool? Maybe he shouldn't even be here, he thought to himself. Who else did not know William had an older son from his first marriage to his mother? Leonard wondered.

Just then Meta came over and interrupted his dark thoughts.

"Leonard, when we get back to the house, could you and I have a few minutes alone?" she asked.

"Certainly," he responded stiffly, assuming the worst and thinking he'd soon be back to eating dinner in the kitchen with the help.

Later at the house, Meta asked him to join her in the library. As they sat looking at each other for a long minute, he recognized genuine sadness in her eyes. For the first time, he felt the beginnings of a bond that he had never felt before. Her loss was the same as his loss, he reasoned, and here they found commonality.

Meta broke the ice. "Leonard, I know you and I have never been very close, but I want you to know that I do love you. You're William's son, and he loved you more than you ever realized.

"From the time we were first married, and throughout our entire lives together, he was always speaking of how much he loved and missed you. And I must confess that sometimes it even made me a little jealous of you."

Leonard listened in amazement.

She continued, "He had a hard decision to make after your mother died, as you know. And he always wondered if it was the right one. But in recent years he confided to me that when he saw what a fine, successful man and father you had become, he knew it was the best decision.

"He was very proud of the man you have become...even

though he always had to give Lulie all the credit." Meta laughed softly at this, and the tension broke between them.

They were both teary-eyed, so Leonard spoke up to thank Meta for her kind words. "That means an awful lot to me. I know you made Dad very happy, which also means a lot to me." He didn't know what else to say.

Meta then reached over for some documents on a side table near the sofa. "Your father left a will, and here is a copy for you."

Leonard leafed through the bundle of papers.

"As you will see, he has generously provided for you, as well as for me and my children. Additionally, a few months ago he told me that if anything ever happened to him, there were three personal items he wanted to be sure that you have."

She rose to her feet and stood behind his father's desk, reaching for a framed painting that was leaning against the desk drawers. She brought the painting to Leonard and laid it in his arms.

"Leonard, your mother painted this after their honeymoon to Scotland. It is quite good, but your father always kept it in the closet, out of respect for me, I guess. He wanted you to have it."

He saw his mother's feathery signature in the lower righthand corner: *Abbie Kellogg, November 27, 1890.* Leonard could not believe he was holding the only tangible memory of his mother. There were no photographs of Abbie that anyone could find. He did not even know what she looked like. But here was something from her past that she had touched.

"The second item your father wanted you to have is his rifle," Meta said as she pointed to a rifle in the corner, enclosed in a case. It was a familiar sight for Leonard, as he'd often admired it throughout the years.

"As you know, it's a Winchester Model 1873 that he purchased the year after your birth. You've probably heard him tell that story of shooting a charging bear a thousand times."

Leonard smiled at the memory.

"And finally," Meta continued as she reached inside a small handbag and presented a small gold coin ring to Leonard.

Leonard recognized it immediately as the ring his father wore on his pinky finger.

"He said you were always fascinated by this ring when you were a baby," Meta explained. "Your father remembered your tiny hands playing with it, so it was something he wanted you to have and remember him by. I want to give these things to you now so you can take them back to Texas with you. Maybe someday you can give them to your son, your dad's namesake."

Leonard did not know what to make of all of this, but he thanked Meta and promised he would take good care of each gift. They walked together back to the living area where many people remained. He spent another hour greeting guests and making small talk but was anxious to return home.

On the train ride back to Texas, Leonard took out his father's will and began to read. William left most his estate in trust for Meta to live off the income for the rest of her life and then be disbursed to each of his four children, including him. This arrangement made sense to Leonard, and he wouldn't really give it much thought until eight years later when Meta died on August 24, 1938, and was laid to rest next to his father's grave in Lakewood Park Cemetery.

When Leonard got home from his father's funeral and showed Esther his mother's oil painting of Fingal's Cave, they both remarked what good shape it was in, especially having been kept in a closet for 40 years. After they had it reframed, he hung the painting prominently in their living room.

Leonard caught himself staring at the piece many nights as he sat in his favorite chair listening to the radio and enjoying one of his fine Cuban cigars. Why had his grandmother painted this particular cave in Scotland? The aura of the mysterious painting haunted him. His father had never talked much about Abbie—where she grew up, her parents, or her childhood. All of Leonard's life he'd felt somewhat unmoored, like a ship drifting alone in the ocean his mother had painted. Who was Abbie, and what was she like? He had no idea where to begin finding any answers, but at least he had her painting.

FORT WORTH, TEXAS 1940

Leonard kept the missing gaps of his past private, confessing only to Esther how much he longed to know more about his mother and her family. In 1940, ten years after his father's death, some legal issues related to the probate of his father's extensive estate arose. Leonard was asked to provide proof of his US citizenship, as there were no official records of him having been born in the United States.

He had never been confronted with this issue before, but now he needed legal proof of who his parents were, their citizenships, and his birth. These questions were things Leonard had wanted to know for years. He wished he'd asked his father more about his mother, but he hadn't. Now no one was left to explain if both his mother, as well as his father, were United States citizens living in Canada at the time of his birth. No one in the family, including him, knew where Abbie was even born or raised.

With his parents and Lulie deceased, he sought help from Fred and Lottie. He wrote Lottie requesting a copy of a certificate from the Fowler School to prove he had attended school in Fall River. Fred also signed an affidavit attesting to the fact that he knew Leonard had been born in Toronto, Canada, his mother had died in childbirth, and that Fred's mother, Lulie, had raised him in their home in Fall River. Outside of those facts, Fred and Lottie knew surprisingly very little about Abbie.

It was perplexing to Leonard that his mother seemed to have disappeared from the pages of family history. Odder still, despite his repeated letters of inquiry, Canadian officials could not find any record of Leonard's birth in 1892.

Leonard wrote Louise, who suggested that perhaps Abbie had met William in Providence, Rhode Island, when he attended Brown University. She replied to Leonard's questions:

> *I am pretty sure your mother came from Providence where Dad met her when he was at Brown University. You might write the courthouse in Providence to get some information about Abbie*

C. Kellogg. The marriage certificate might be reg-
istered there.

I might take a wild guess that Dad and your
mother were married about the year 1890 or so.
Mother and Dad were married, I think, in 1895.
It's bad enough to lose track of the Davis family
but losing your own mother's family entirely is
pretty bad and a darned shame.

Louise thought she'd heard family tales through the years
to that effect, but that assumption turned out to be a rabbit
trail leading nowhere. In all likelihood, not much was ever
said in her mother's household about William's first marriage
to Abbie.

For her part, Lottie was willing to go through old boxes of
letters, having remembered once seeing a handwritten letter
from Abbie to Lulie after she and William had first married. She shared her recollection of what it said in a letter to
Leonard. It read in part:

I have a letter somewhere written to my mother by
your mother just before you were born. I will see if
I can find it and send it to you. My mother loved
your mother more than I can tell. I remember her

faintly and know that she was very lovely. You get
all of your inherited hell from your dad!

Lottie was unsuccessful in finding the letter, but after doing more digging and research in family albums, she wrote Leonard again.

Your dad and mother were married in Toronto. I
think she had a brother, Billy Kellogg, who may
be living. You had a great-grandfather named
Cassidy who called you "Little Jesus Christ" after
you were born, no one else ever said it though.

Now, when I get the date of your graduation from
Fowler, that will finish up what information I can
give you.

Much love to Esther and Bill and absent Bob.

Yours in the usual haste,
Lottie

Billy Kellogg—now that was a name Leonard had heard before. He vaguely remembered his father mentioning Abbie's younger brother who had lived with them the summer before Leonard was born. He recalled his father saying how incorrigible the boy had been with his own father, William Kellogg. But he'd been no trouble when he lived with them in their tiny apartment. Was Willie still alive? Leonard wasn't sure. Maybe his mother had other siblings he could contact.

In another letter, Louise tried to mollify him by assuring Leonard that he was from "good stock," which he appreciated since he had very little else to go on. Still, Leonard remained undeterred and fascinated to find out more about his past.

In the fall of 1940, he wrote the registrar in Toronto asking for a copy of Abbie's death certificate, which he received after Christmas. He'd gone to the mailbox earlier that morning, expecting a backlog of mail and the regular circulars inside after the holidays. To his surprise, he saw a packet stamped in the return address window: Province of Ontario, Dominion of Canada.

"Esther?" he called to his wife as he walked inside and set the packet on the kitchen table. "You might want to see this."

Esther came into the kitchen carrying a stack of folded dishcloths. "What is it, Leonard? Did we win something?" she joked, pulling up a chair beside him.

"You might say that," Leonard said.

He pulled out of the packet a thin stack of documents printed on very official-looking paper. Leonard carefully read the cover letter before revealing a worn and yellowed piece of paper that he immediately recognized as his original birth certificate.

He stared at the names of his mother and father and tentatively reached out to trace his mother's name with his finger:

ABBIE C. KELLOGG
Born: Peoria, Illinois, United States of America

"See? Didn't I tell you that you would find it, Leonard?" Esther said as she rubbed his shoulder.

Leonard longed to have more, but it would have to wait, perhaps even beyond what his lifetime would allow. Perhaps someone in his lineage would someday share the same longing to know more about his mother, and additional facts would finally come to light.

⊹⊱══◉ ◉══⊰⊹

Esther and Leonard focused on raising Bill and Bob to become men of hard work, courage, and integrity, never allowing life to weigh them down by its challenges. They had one great helper in raising their boys, Ada Williams. Ada was a young African American woman who came to work for them when Bill was just three years old. She loved Bill and Bob as if they were her own and was in a very real sense a second mother to them all their lives.

Ada was very much part of the family. So much so that even after Leonard and Esther's deaths, Bill and his wife, Virginia, would continue to employee Ada into her final years. She loved and doted on their children, Linda and Leonard, as she had done with Bill and Bob. When Ada passed in 1976, the Davis family lost a dear and loyal friend who had helped love and nurture three generations of Davis's for over 50 years.

Bill and Bob inherited the calm demeanor and good nature of their father, along with the determination of Esther, their mother. The two boys grew up with different interests and passions, but both had a technical and engineering-focused mind. Engineering was in Leonard's blood, just as it had been in his father's, and he passed down that interest to both his sons. However, it was Bill who turned out to be most interested in the electrical industry. He followed in his father's footsteps and joined the same company formerly named Fort Worth Light & Power that was now the Texas Electric Service Company (TESCO). Bill began working on June 1, 1937—25 years to the day after Leonard had first joined the company on June 1, 1912. As a hobby, Bill was also a very talented artist, a trait he inherited from his grandmother Abbie.

Bill attended Texas Christian University in Fort Worth his

first year out of high school, but like his father he ultimately went to work rather than spending more time in school. As his father had done for him, Leonard helped Bill get started on the bottom rung of the ladder, working in the mail room for the electric company. And like his father, Bill was a quick study. Within six months, he moved to the meter department reading electric meters outside customers' houses.

It was not a glamourous job and more than once he wondered if he should have stayed in college. Nevertheless, Bill saved his money for a future that he hoped would one day include getting married and having a family. Two years into his work, Bill met a beautiful young lady named Virginia Francis Roberts (1917-2010) who was a typist for Dun & Bradstreet.

Virginia's mother, Agnes Rebecca Mason Roberts (1884-1967), reminded Leonard of Esther's hard-working family. Agnes' husband, Watson Mearle Roberts (1885-1931), died in 1931 at the age of 46, leaving her with three children to raise on her own. They had a tough time of it. Agnes had graduated with a teaching degree from Miami University in Oxford, Ohio, in 1903 and had worked as a teacher. But she felt she needed to stay home after the death of her husband so she could concentrate on raising her children and never returned to work as a teacher.

Funds were tight, but one day a close friend from church encouraged Agnes to invest her only asset, a $1,000 life insurance proceed, into an oil well venture with Amoco Oil Company in Oklahoma. The well was successful, and its modest royalty helped provide her with just enough income to get by for many years. When Virginia graduated from high school, she went straight to work to help her mother financially so that her older siblings, Marie Adeline Roberts (1910-1968) and Watson Mearle Roberts, Jr. (1914-1994), could continue attending Texas Christian University. Virginia put her own college dream aside to help ensure her brother and sister were able to graduate, which they did.

Bill and Virginia fell in love and married on March 13, 1941, in Agnes' living room at 2905 Lipscomb Street in Fort Worth. After the couple returned from their honeymoon in Oklahoma City, they moved into their first apartment at 601 Parkdale and resumed their respective jobs. The newlyweds were happy and excited about the future. But dark clouds were gathering in Europe.

⊷⊶⊙⊷⊶

FORT WORTH, TEXAS
December 1941

Eight months after their wedding, Bill and Virginia arrived to pick up her mother for church on Sunday morning December

7, 1941. When they knocked on her door, her mother swiftly waved them inside and said, "You all come on into the living room. You've got to hear this."

As they entered, she turned to the large wooden radio standing in the corner and motioned for Bill and Virginia to sit down. The news anchor for the National Mutual Radio Network breathlessly announced, "Word has just reached us that the Japanese have attacked Pearl Harbor in a massive air assault. Heavy casualties are being reported."

Bill stared at Virginia, who began to weep.

"Oh my God," she sobbed. "Now we are sure to be in the middle of this horrible war." Her mother reached over for her daughter's hand.

"Honey, I lived through World War I," she assured her. "Your father fought in it, and we survived it. We will survive this one as well. Now, let's go on to church and give this to the Lord."

The church was packed at University Methodist on Berry Street by the time Bill, Virginia, and her mother arrived. The entire congregation joined with the rest of a scared and uneasy nation in asking for God's protection and strength.

The next evening Bill and Virginia went to his parents' house for dinner. Bill, Virginia, Leonard, Esther, and Bill's younger brother, Bob, all gathered around the radio after dinner to listen to President Roosevelt's address to the nation.

None would ever forget when President Roosevelt called the attack on Pearl Harbor "a date that will live in infamy." With those words, everyone knew their lives and the lives of all Americans would never be the same again. The next day the United States Congress unanimously approved a Declaration of War against Japan and three days later against Germany. World War II had begun.

⋆⟫⊜ ⊜⟪⋆

Like most young men in America, Bill and Bob were eager to join up and "give it back to the Nazis and Japs." Since the war had been brewing in Europe and the Pacific for several years, Bill and many others anticipated that it would only be a matter of time before it would draw in America. Bill had already made application to join the Army Air Force a few months prior to the attack on Pearl Harbor, and his application was still pending. He even took a two-month Radio Code course at Technical High School in Fort Worth in the fall to better prepare himself for his possible service.

Bob soon followed suit and applied to the Army Air Force a few months later. They both wanted to be pilots. In the fall of 1942 Bill and Bob finally received notice that both had been accepted as Aviation Cadets with the Army Air Force. The brothers were ecstatic. They were going to learn to be pilots, serve their country, and repay those who had dared threatened America's very way of life.

Virginia, however, was not as enthusiastic. A young bride, she was filled with fear and apprehension, as were Esther and Leonard who had both lived through World War I. They knew the horrors of war and felt it posed a real risk that one or both of their sons might never come back from overseas. Nevertheless, the boys were like thousands of other young men their age, chomping at the bit to join the fight.

Bob was called up first and Bill a few weeks later. Bob trained at Blackland Airfield in Waco, Texas, and Bill at the Kelly Airfield in San Antonio, Texas. Bob took to flying like a duck to water, but Bill could never nail his landings quite to his instructor's liking and was soon washed out as a pilot.

Bill was devastated and felt like a failure who was not only letting his country down but also his family. Virginia tried to encourage him when he came home on leave, but it didn't help his bruised ego. Finally, one evening at his parents' house after dinner, his father asked him to join him on their screened-in porch.

After sharing one of his favorite Cuban cigars with his son, Leonard said, "Look, son, I know you are terribly disappointed.

And I don't blame you one bit. I've been in the same place you are many times in my life, and I will tell you what my father told me. When you get knocked down, you have to get back up and keep going."

He continued, "Life is full of disappointments and failures, but it is what we make of those things that counts. We can let them defeat us, or we can make them motivate us. It's your choice. There are many ways to serve your country, you know. It takes more than pilots to run an air force."

"I know, Dad," Bill said.

"Grit your teeth and find out where and how you can best serve, other than flying a dadgum airplane."

"You're right. I'll do that. I promise you," Bill conceded.

Leonard smiled. Then he blew a smoke ring, grabbed his son's arm and said, "I'm so proud of you, Bill. You are a good son and fine husband. Your mother and I love you with all our heart, and we'll be praying for you every day."

⋅⊷⊷⊷⊷⋅

During the war, Leonard and Esther's story was like so many American families who prayed for their sons' safe return and a swift end to the horrible conflict. They treasured letters from their boys and traded the limited information they were able to share of their whereabouts with other members of the family who wrote and called to ask how they were doing.

Bill took his dad's encouragement to heart and served in the Army Air Force for three years. He found his niche in radios, as well as the newest innovation of the day—radar. His superiors quickly recognized his technical skills and put him to work installing, maintaining, and operating the latest radio and radar equipment the Air Force was using to win the war. He was initially based in Scott Field, Illinois, and then in Boca Taron, Florida. Later, he also served aboard the U.S. Larkspur, a hospital ship making runs to Europe to bring back wounded soldiers. Onboard he maintained and operated radar equipment to detect enemy planes.

Bill was a recipient of the American Theater Campaign Medal and World War II Victory Medal. Virginia moved in with her mother in his absence, volunteered for the Red Cross, wrote letters to her husband every day, and read each morning's newspaper with eager anticipation of any sign the war might be ending soon.

Bob served in the Army Air Force as a pilot flying B-17 bombing raids out of England into the heart of Nazi Germany throughout the war. Although the enemy frequently shot up his plane, Bob was never shot down. Once he had to make an emergency crash landing in England due to the extensive damage to his plane. When both of their sons returned from the war unscathed, Leonard and Esther shared in the joy of millions of Americans who celebrated the Allied victory in Europe and the safe return of their loved ones.

As part of the demobilization after the war ended, Bill was honorably discharged on February 26, 1946, at Camp Fannin in Tyler, Texas. He was 28 years old and returned home to Virginia and their now two-year-old daughter, Linda Kay, born October 29, 1943. He'd missed so much during Linda's first two years and determined to make it up to the cutest little girl a father could ever want.

Bill also returned to his job at TESCO, but not to his old job in the meter department. With the radio and radar skills he had acquired in the Air Force, Bill was given responsibility over TESCO's newest innovation—the installation, maintenance, and training of employees in the use of two-way radios in its line trucks. He continued with TESCO for the next 36 years, advancing to Sub-station and Communications Foreman, then to the General Office of Engineering working as an Electrical Engineer. A few years after his discharge from the Army, Bill and Virginia had a second child on January 15, 1948. They named him after his grandfather, Leonard Ellsworth Davis.

After he returned from the war, Bill's brother, Bob, completed his studies at the University of Oklahoma where he met and married his wife, Patricia Ann Barron (1926-1982). They soon headed West to California, and he graduated from Stanford University with a degree in Mechanical Engineering, following in his father and grandfather's footsteps as engineers. He was an aerospace engineer in the Gemini and Apollo space programs and later worked on classified winged aircraft projects.

Bob continued to fly throughout his life and served in the Air Force Reserves, retiring in 1974 as a Lieutenant Colonel. He and Pat had three children: Brian Ellsworth Davis born July 20, 1956, Elizabeth "Libby" Scott Davis born April 11, 1958, and Wendy Jean Davis born August 17, 1962. Pat died on October 22, 1982, and Bob died October 17, 1989, at the age of 62.

⋅⊶⊷⋅

Leonard and Esther doted on their five grandchildren. Over the years, they made several trips from Texas to California to see Bob's family. They spent time with Bill and Virginia and their two children on a regular basis since they lived in the same town. Friday nights were always special, as the family tradition included Leonard taking Bill, Virginia, and the kids to Wyatt's Cafeteria for dinner.

The electric power business was in the Davis family for over 100 years. At the pinnacle of his career, Leonard served as the Commercial Sales Manager for TESCO. Since the time he joined the company in 1912 he'd been at the forefront of company expansion of its electric service business, ultimately stretching all the way from Fort Worth to Wichita Falls to Midland-Odessa in far West Texas. Leonard played a pivotal role in seeing TESCO become one of the predominate electric utilities in the entire Southwest, just as his father had predicted when he addressed the Fort Worth Commission back in 1910.

TESCO showed Leonard its appreciation in his 36th year of service by paying for a well-deserved and much-needed extended vacation to the northeastern United States. He and Esther visited Chicago, the Great Lakes, and then on to the East Coast to see the remaining members of Leonard's family, Lottie and Fred. They traveled by ship across Lake Michigan from Chicago, ending up in upper Michigan at Mackinaw Island for the afternoon on their way to Canada.

After that they headed back to Detroit by train. Leonard imagined he was riding over the same tracks from Cleveland to Detroit that his father had built when he was Superintendent of the Lorain & Cleveland Electric Railway 50 years earlier. From Detroit, the couple made their way to Atlantic City, New

Jersey, where they stayed at the Marlborough-Blenheim Hotel near the Jersey Shore's famous Boardwalk. It was wonderful being right on the ocean, seeing and smelling a different way of life.

They then journeyed to Fall River to see Lottie and her family. It had been many years since Leonard had left his hometown. He enjoyed showing Esther where he had grown up, and he took her by Fowler school. They drove past his grandparents' house and even made a visit to Oak Grove Cemetery to pay his respects to his Aunt Lulie and both his grandparents.

They were then on to New York where they visited all the usual tourist destinations and had their fill of fine food. They met up with Fred and his wife, Menta, at Jones Beach on Long Island where they shared a wonderful dinner. It was a trip of a lifetime and brought Leonard full circle to where he had started. However, when they arrived home after the long journey, they were both relieved and exhausted. Esther was able to give her two grandchildren special gifts she had purchased just for them in New York, and Leonard returned to the office much-refreshed and thankful to his superiors for such a thoughtful gift.

Leonard continued to serve out his career with TESCO for another 14 years until his retirement in 1962 at the age of

70 on his 50ᵗʰ anniversary with the company. When he was presented with his 50-year service award, his son, Bill, also received his 25-year service award and was well on his way to completing a lifelong career with TESCO.

Leonard and Esther grew old together, living in the same house at 3431 Avenue J for the rest of their days. They enjoyed a rich and meaningful life that was better than either could have ever imagined. But from time to time, Leonard's mind drifted back to his days in Fall River. Sometimes he even imagined his journey as a newborn in his father's arms from Toronto to Fall River. His father had done all he could for him, not knowing that his efforts would be rewarded for generations to come.

⋅⊱══⊰ ⊱══⊰⋅

TORONTO, CANADA 1948

In 1948 when Leonard and Esther were on vacation in the Northeast, they made a special side trip across the border to Toronto, Canada, where Leonard was born 56 years earlier. He had something special that he wanted to see.

Standing at his mother's weathered gravestone in Mount Pleasant Cemetery, he brushed the leaves and dirt away and read the engraved words slowly:

ABBIE
BELOVED WIFE OF
W.E. DAVIS
DIED MAY 21ST, 1892
18 YEARS, SIX MONTHS, 21 DAYS

It had been fifty-six years since Abbie had given him the gift of life on May 21, 1892. Fifty-six years since he'd laid in her arms in the hospital. Fifty-six years since his father, William, had beamed at Abbie, both smiling proudly into the face of their son as they dreamed of their future together as a family. And fifty-six years since their dream shattered a few hours later when she left behind her husband and baby. Standing there in silence, Leonard felt for the first time that he finally knew his mother and her enduring love for him. Tears came easily as Leonard thanked Abbie for her sacrifice. Abbie had given him life and at the same time had given life to generations upon generations who would carry her seed with them and theirs forever.

EPILOGUE

In May 2023, I retraced William and Abbie's 1890 honeymoon trip to Scotland. Rather than a steamship, my wife, Rhonda and I flew to Edinburgh and then traveled by car to the Isle of Erska. From Erska, we took a ferry the next morning to the Isle of Mull, drove two hours to the opposite end, then took another ferry to the Isle of Iona, the birthplace of Christianity in Scotland in 563 A.D. After visiting the ruins of the Iona Abbey and eating the best fish & chips ever from a food truck on the dock, we boarded a small tour boat to take us to the Isle of Staffa.

As the boat bobbed with the ocean swells, I saw what Abbie had seen and painted 133 years before. Fingal's Cave looked exactly like her painting, except for the two lone figures she had placed on the clifftop staring into the distance. I felt a gentle satisfaction having somewhat solved the mystery of Fingal's Cave, the story of the young woman who had painted it, and the lives of those who came before and after her.

The endeavor ended up being much more complicated than I initially thought. My desire to know more about my family history started as a genealogy project, but as I researched more deeply, it became much more than that. I found people who had suffered multiple tragedies and had overcome them to live meaningful and productive lives. I found love and heartbreak, success and failure, happiness and grief. My journey became much more than just filling out a family tree or trying to see if you were related to someone on the Mayflower. It was about discovering and trying to understand the lives my family lived during their time in history.

At the suggestion of my friend and writing consultant, Mary Ann Lackland, I decided to convert my research into a historical fiction novel. I hope that it will give my children, and their children, and their children's children—and perhaps others—a fun, interesting, and meaningful glimpse into the lives of those who came before them and help inform those who come after us.

The story covers some 200 years of the lives of two American families from the early 1800s to the early 2000s.

Their lives were much like those who experienced the growth and maturing of our country. Their history covered the Civil War, Westward expansion, the silver and gold mining booms and busts, and the myriad of innovations including the steamship, harnessing electric power, railroads, the telephone, and the automobile. Their story was also interwoven with the tragedies of World War I, the Great Depression, and World War II.

Abbie's Sacrifice begins with Leonard's birth and ends with his death, but more of the story is still being written. In fact, I came across something written by Fred Smith, my friend and the Founder of The Gathering. Fred captures my hopes for this book much better than I ever could. He writes:

> *"Our lives are connected to those who came before and those who follow. We are not a collection of independent short stories. There is no disconnected individual journey. Our lives are chapters in a novel whose author has woven us together to accomplish His purpose – one life at a time."*

My own chapter is nearing its end, but my hope is that it, along with the family chapters chronicled here, will help inform what's yet to be written by those who follow.

Writing this story has been one of the most interesting,

challenging, and rewarding things I have ever done. I had done a fair amount of legal writing and research during my legal career, but I had never done any creative writing. I found it fascinating and captivating. I have gotten so lost for hours upon hours in my research and writing that my wife would keep telling me, "Take a break," to which I would reply, "In a minute, in a minute." But my research and writing would turn into hours.

I have no idea how much time has gone into this endeavor because the time just flew by unnoticed. We've had a lot of fun with it as well. Rhonda and I located Judge Kellogg's family plot in Oakwood Cemetery in Leadville, Colorado. The Judge, Abbie, and their infant son, Leonard, are all buried there, along with their oldest daughter, Pauline. We are in the process of replacing worn headstones and sprucing up the plot. We were also surprised to learn that their family home at 130 West Ninth Street in Leadville is still standing, and we even managed to tour it.

On a recent business trip to Boston, we also took a couple of extra days to see Fall River where my great-grandfather William was raised. There we visited Oak Grove Cemetery and saw the graves of Leonard's Nana and PaPa, his Aunt Lulie, and his adopted siblings, Lottie and Fred. We drove by their houses on South Beach Street where they lived. Rhonda and I even spent one creepy night at the Lizzie Borden House where the infamous axe murders occurred in 1892. (For an extra twenty-five dollars, I had housekeeping place a red-handled rubber hatchet under Rhonda's pillow, which caused much excitement as she retired to bed!) As of this writing, we hope to travel soon to Toronto to see Abbie's grave and then go on to Cleveland where William Ellsworth Davis worked and is buried.

Today Rhonda and I live at the base of Mt. Princeton near Buena Vista, Colorado. It is less than three miles from Mt. Princeton Hot Springs where Abbie's father, the Judge, sought the medicinal benefits of the natural geothermal springs in an attempt to deal with his crippling rheumatism. Back then it was known as Heywood Springs. One thing I've learned since living in this area is how important the silver boom was in Colorado. The Judge helped manage the financing of many mining endeavors when he lived in Leadville, and I was amazed to learn that over $2.5 billion in today's dollars was mined in silver throughout Colorado during the silver boom.

As for the rest of the members of Abbie's family, I'm afraid my research indicates that heartbreak continued to follow Abbie's siblings after her untimely death. After living in Peoria with her grandmother and aunt, Pauline eventually migrated to Washington state. She made good on her promise to remain single and ultimately died in California at the age of 70 in 1942 alone, never marrying or having children. She did, however, leave behind instructions that she wished to be buried in Oakwood Cemetery in Leadville, Colorado, next to her mother, baby brother Leonard, and her father.

Willie also continued to struggle after Abbie's death. What I could find out about his story is that he dropped out of military school a few months after his sister's funeral. I imagine that Willie could no longer focus on his studies and was very depressed after the loss of both his mother and sister. I do have a copy of a letter his father, the Judge, wrote to his sister Lou about Willie's situation a few weeks after Abbie's death.

Dear Lou,

I am thinking of sending Willie up to your country, if you and Ma think best, and if you could make room for him during his vacations. I received from Pauline a catalogue of Tacoma School in Washington and she said she would find out about one in Seattle.

Do you know anything about them? I must send Willie somewhere, and I don't want him here in

Leadville. If you are all agreeable, I will have him
go direct to Tacoma.

After leaving military school in Michigan and completing school in Tacoma, Washington, Willie went back to Toronto in 1894 to meet up with old friends. He met a young woman there, Elizabeth Nicholson, and they married quickly when Willie was just 18. They had one son, William Frank Kellogg Jr, in 1895. By the following year, Willie was retracing his roots and living in Peoria working as a laborer. He bounced around various states in the Midwest including Ohio, Indiana, Illinois, and Michigan throughout his life. Ultimately, he followed Pauline in his later years to California where he died at the age of 80 in Los Angeles.

Today, Abbie's painting of Fingal's Cave hangs over the fireplace in our home in Buena Vista, Colorado, just as it did in William and Abbie's home in Toronto until he took it down after her death and replaced it with his Winchester Model 1873 rifle. The Winchester he used to shoot the charging bear was left to my grandfather, then to my father, and then to me. I have now handed it down to my son, who will leave this priceless treasure one day to his son.

I have worn William's one dollar gold piece ring for many years, and I still have PaPa's old toolbox that now serves as a coffee table in our home. The vintage woodworking tools that William left for my grandfather now proudly hang on a wall above the workbench in my shop. Also, the small oil royalty that Virginia's mother purchased after her husband's early death continued to pay modest monthly royalties to my grandmother, my mother, my sister and me, and now to our children. It's not a lot, but it is interesting to realize that something purchased out of a tragedy in 1931 during the Great Depression is still a blessing to members of our family almost 100 years later.

In addition to these physical items, many traits and talents have carried over from Abbie and William to those who have followed in their footsteps. William's engineering acumen carried over to his son, Leonard, and to both of his grandsons, Bill and Bob. My father, Bill, then passed it on to my sister and to me. Linda and I both majored in mathematics and worked as computer programmers and system analysts after college.

For most of my life, I thought I was the only one in my family with an interest in the law. Now I like to think that it was the Judge's acumen for the law that may have helped me become a successful lawyer and later a judge. Two of my sons are lawyers as well. I think Abbie would be proud to know that her artistic talents also carried over to my father, who was a very accomplished artist in his late teens, just as she was. In fact, several of my father's paintings hang on the walls of our home. Many of my children are very artistic and creative as well.

Something I noticed during my research of our family tree is how essential William and the Judge's affable and engaging personalities were to their success. I could tell by reading their obituaries how much they enjoyed people and vice versa. That trait was then evident in Leonard and his grandson, Bill, and it's something in their personalities that I remember with great fondness. My father died in 2001 at the age of 83. My mother, Virginia, died in 2010 at the age of 92. Both were wonderful parents who worked hard to provide their children a happy middleclass upbringing filled with love, faith in God, and devotion to family. My sister and I are both blessed to have had them as parents.

My sister, Linda Kay Lewis, (1943 -) retired as a computer system executive for an insurance company and now lives in Mansfield, Texas. She has two children, Marcus and Barbara. Marcus Lewis (1971-) is head of security at Southwestern Medical Center in Dallas. He and his wife, Tammi, live in Mansfield as well. They also have two children, Reagan and Dylan. Reagan is a pre-med student at North Texas State University in Denton. Dylan is a varsity swimmer at Mansfield high school. Barbara Lewis Curtis (1969 -) and her husband,

Kendall, live in Savannah, Texas, and have two children, Maddy and Kalel.

I have five children. William Ellsworth Davis III (1976 -) is a trial attorney specializing in intellectual property law disputes. He and his wife, Annie, live in Crested Butte, Colorado, and have four children: Cy, Brody, Ella, and Addie.

Stafford Grigsby Helm Davis (1978 -) and his wife, Ashley, live in Tyler, Texas, and have two children: Ford and Lee. Stafford is a trial attorney with a general civil practice.

Blake Twyman Davis LaMarca (1980 -) lives in Katonah, New York, where she has her own private chef business. She has two children: Grayson and Emmerson.

Lindsey Austin Davis Reed (1982 -) lives in Dallas, Texas, and negotiates arbitration disputes between insurance companies. She has one son named Howard.

DeWhitte Hawkins Davis (1984 -) lives in Dallas, Texas, and does cyber-security work for the federal government.

If Abbie and William are looking down from heaven, I hope they see that Abbie's sacrifice created and passed on their unique traits, gifts, and personalities to their son, two grandchildren, five great-grandchildren, and eight great-great-grandchildren, and even to their 13 great-great-great-grandchildren.

It's true. Our lives are all intertwined as *"chapters in a novel whose author has woven us together to accomplish His purpose – one life at a time."* May each chapter be a good one with a happy ending.

Leonard Ellsworth Davis

ABOUT THE AUTHOR

Judge Leonard Ellsworth Davis is a retired United States District Judge for the Eastern District of Texas. He graduated from the University of Texas at Arlington in 1970 with a degree in mathematics and worked several years as a computer programmer and systems analyst for Texas Electric Service Company in Fort Worth, Texas. Judge Davis obtained a master's degree in management science from Texas Christian University, then graduated first in his class from Baylor University School of Law and served as Editor-in-Chief of the *Baylor Law Review*.

The next 23 years he was a partner and trial attorney with the Potter-Minton law firm in Tyler, Texas, until his appointment as Chief Judge of the Twelfth Court of Appeals of the State of Texas. In 2002 President George W. Bush nominated and the United States Senate confirmed his appointment to the

United States District Court for the Eastern District of Texas. He also served by invitation on the United States Courts of Appeal for the Federal Circuit in Washington, D.C. and the Fifth Circuit in New Orleans, Louisiana. During his tenure on the bench, Judge Davis oversaw one of the largest intellectual property law dockets in the country. He retired from the bench in 2015 but continues to provide strategic counseling for clients involved in worldwide intellectual property law disputes for the international intellectual property law firm of Fish & Richardson in Boston.

Judge Davis and his wife, Rhonda, share their time between Tyler, Texas, and Buena Vista, Colorado. While he lived and worked most of his life in East Texas, the mountains of Colorado always called to him. It's where he enjoyed many backpacking adventures with his children and summiting 27 of Colorado's 14,000-foot peaks. He spent countless hours rafting and fishing the Arkansas River and chasing the elk, deer, and mountain goats of Colorado. Judge Davis has five children and nine grandchildren spread across the country from Texas, to New York, to Colorado, who are all frequent and welcome visitors to their home in Colorado.

Books by Leonard Ellsworth Davis

Abbie's Sacrifice: A Novel

Requiem: Poems and Musings of William Ellsworth Davis

Available on Amazon.com

Made in the USA
Coppell, TX
04 December 2024

41773838R00152